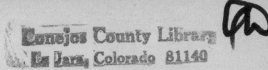

TROUBLE ON THE TRAIL

Pete took off the jacket and tied it onto the back of the saddle with the bundle of clothes for Rosy. The slicker was back at camp. He looked at the sky again. Thunderstorms didn't blow up so quickly at this time of year. If there came a rain it was more likely to be a slow, cold one. Still, it always seemed that when a fellow left his slicker in the wagon or back at a camp, that was when he needed it.

He was pulling tight on the leather thongs when he heard a noise at his back. Glancing over his left shoulder, he saw two riders coming from the east. They were less than a hundred yards away. The one on the left was Flagg.

Pete's horse was already looking at the other horses, as was the one he was leading. Pete unwound the lead rope from his saddle horn. Then, trying not to seem in a hurry, he mounted up and waited for the riders to come nearer.

Other *Leisure* books by John D. Nesbitt:
ONE-EYED COWBOY WILD

BLACK DIAMOND RENDEZVOUS

JOHN D. NESBITT

LEISURE BOOKS   NEW YORK CITY

For my brother Bob.

A LEISURE BOOK®

May 1998

Published by

Dorchester Publishing Co., Inc.
276 Fifth Avenue
New York, NY 10001

ISBN 0-8439-4388-2

BLACK DIAMOND DIAMOND RENDEZVOUS

Chapter One

Pete Garnett was scouting below the rimrock when he met the girl. He had never met a girl that way before. The uncommon part was that he found it necessary to kill the two men she was with before he could ask her name or introduce himself. If he had met her in a more usual way, he might have decided that she was not his type of girl, but because of the way things started, he got to know her a little better.

It was early fall. The aspen leaves were turning yellow, and the light breeze made the leaves quake. It was a sunny afternoon, warm with a cool undertone. The good weather carried with it a fragile feeling that floated on the air like a soft voice, warning that the weather could turn cold and bitter any day.

The smell of sage and juniper, dry grass, falling leaf, and dust—sometimes all one smell—reminded a person that the easy times would not be for long. Not that any time was ever really easy—not in the mountains of southeastern Wyoming Territory, where it could snow on any day of the year, or drop forty degrees from breakfast to dinner. But the season from May to October was mild compared to the hard times coming.

As he noticed the aspens, Pete thought of the trees he had passed when he crossed the creek on his way up. The chokecherry leaves were going through their autumn red and into yellow. Just a little more than a month earlier, when he had been through here last, those leaves had been dark green and the long, slender branches had drooped with the ripe fruit. There were no black chokecherries now, just leaves turning color. In years past he had seen broad-leafed trees and bushes—chokecherries and aspen here, or lilacs and elms in town—loaded with snow while the green leaves still clung to the branches. But those were early wet snows that melted off in a day. The hard snows and deep, dangerous cold would come later, when the leaves had run their course and left only bare branches. That was what the leaves spoke of now—the setting in of hard weather, the march of time. The solid greens of summer gave no such hint.

Pete was scouting the country because he was

scheduled to take out a party of Eastern sport hunters in a couple of weeks. Fall roundup had been short. It was only the second fall roundup since the bad winter of 1886–87, and there had not been much to gather or ship. Pete was off the payroll, so he took to the high country while the weather was still smiling. Since he was scouting for deer and elk, he took his time.

The dark horse, Star, knew the difference between chasing cows and stalking game. Star was a good hunting horse as well as a good cow horse. He often spotted wild animals before Pete was aware of them, and when the horse came to a stop as he did now, Pete tuned his senses even sharper.

Although the movement of horse and rider had not made much noise, Pete was able to hear better as soon as Star paused. The breeze that shivered the aspen leaves carried on it a faint sound. To someone like Pete who spent much of his time in the big open, an unidentified sound still carried meaning. Pete could hear a noise and know first whether it was human or animal. They didn't make the same kinds of noises. The sound might turn out to be a deer getting up from its bed, a squirrel jumping from branch to branch, or a man moving through dry leaves, but Pete's first flicker of knowledge was a sense of whether he was in the vicinity of people or still in the natural world. His first impression was usually reliable.

Right now, he knew the noise was human. He

listened. It was not a voice, but it was a sound borne on human breath. It was accompanied by a non-rhythmic sound like a struggle or scuffle—foot against ground, body against body.

Pete laid his hand on the horse's neck, then held the saddle horn as he swung down quietly. He was glad his spurs were in the saddlebag. Standing by the horse, he stroked its neck with the back of his hand. Then he ducked under its head, gathered the reins neat and short with his left hand, and moved forward. His right hand brushed down to touch the pistol and hover there.

The aspen grew in patches in the high country, sometimes on the fringe of and sometimes engulfed by stands of dark timber. The sounds seemed to be coming from a spot where the aspen thicket met the evergreens. Again Pete heard a sound, not quite a voice, and he thought it was a woman's. After tying his horse to an aspen, he stepped forward.

Thirty yards farther, he came to the place where the sounds came from. He paused in the cover of the foliage and looked onto a clearing where the aspens met the pines.

A man with his back to Pete was holding a woman with her arms pinioned. The man was standing with his legs apart, and it looked as if the woman was trying to stomp on his toes. A second man was facing her, and he had a thin smile on his face.

Pete was out of the second man's line of vision. Pete could not see the woman very well—just a head of dark hair—but he could tell what was about to happen. On the man's face there was an expression, a thin smile and a glint in the eyes, that looked wrong. The man unbuckled his belt, unbuttoned his trousers, and spread open the bottom of his shirt. Pete saw a flash of the man's stomach and bare waist, white as a fish's belly, and the sight put a jolt of sick dread through his own upper body.

"Hold it right there," he heard himself say.

The man with the open pants crouched, turned towards Pete, and brought up a six-gun.

Pete's gun was in his hand and firing—once, twice, three times. The man spun, dropping his pistol, and fell to the ground. He didn't move.

Three shots gone—that meant two left. Pete always carried five in the cylinder, so that the hammer was on an empty chamber. The other man was trying to turn the woman to use her as a shield, but she wrenched away. As she did so, Pete saw that her dress, a dark blue, had been pulled up above her waist and was now falling to cover her thighs and legs. She had dark skin, and in the split second between shooting the first man and covering the second, Pete admired the way the skin caught the sun.

"Now you hold it," he snapped. The second man stood frozen as the woman turned away and bent to rearrange herself.

On the other side of the clearing, farther to Pete's left, there was motion in the thicket. Then came the noise of horses breaking away. Pete kept his gaze focused on the man standing in front of him, but he registered the woman to his right and the commotion to his left.

He moved forward, his gun leveled at the man. "I've got three shots left," he said, knowing that the other man would have figured him for that many. "Don't make me use any of them." He flicked a glance at the man on the ground, who lay motionless. Then he looked hard at the man who was still standing. The man was not wearing a gun, but his right hand hung as if he was used to carrying one. He was looking back at Pete, his features like rock.

"Don't be too sure of yourself," the man said.

"I'm not. But I know what was going on. And it's not going any farther."

"You're not going to kill me," the man said, in a tone somewhere between a taunt and a command.

"You don't know that yet. But if you do as you're told, you'll do better than your partner."

The man's right hand relaxed.

Pete motioned with his gun. "Pull his pants up and button them."

The other man drew his brows together in a question.

"Get his pants up. There's a lady present."

"Ah, she's just a—"

"You heard me. Get him covered up proper."

The man nodded and moved.

Pete moved to his left to keep a good line of

vision. Then he realized he hadn't seen where the dead man's pistol landed. Pete edged farther to the left as the other man knelt in front of his dead partner, blocking Pete's view of all but his back. Pete stepped again to the left, and as he did, the other man whipped around in a crouch and fired a shot at the spot where Pete had been. Pete's six-gun bucked in his hand and sent a shot into the center of the crouched target. He jumped again to his left, in case the man had it in him to place another shot, but the man didn't. He lay sprawled across the body of his partner.

Pete shook his head and swallowed. It had all happened so quickly. As he looked at the dead man, slumped and covering the other man's shame, he said, "Should've done what he was told." The body gave a spasm and Pete jerked, but he held his fire. Then all was still.

He turned and looked at the woman. She looked back at him, stone-faced, and then she looked at his gun. He put it in the holster, rolling his lips back against his teeth and raising his eyebrows.

"Are you all right?" he asked.

"I think so," she answered. With her right hand she pushed a thick strand of her long black hair over her shoulder. She had pretty skin and a smooth neck. She was not very old.

As Pete was absorbing these impressions, he noticed she wore a small silver crucifix suspended from a white cord around her neck. In his mind he moved through that detail and back to the moment at hand. "Do you, or did you, know these two?" He frowned and motioned towards the two dead men. "I know I've never seen either of them before."

"I barely met them."

Up until this point he had supposed the girl was either Indian or Mexican, and now from the tone of her last statement he imagined she was Mexican. That fit with the crucifix.

"My name's Pete," he said. "Pete Garnett."

"My name is Rosa María Peña." She dipped her head forward, as if by habit.

Pete touched his hat brim. "Pleased to meet you. Under the circumstances." He grimaced.

She gave him a questioning look.

"I mean, I'm sorry we had to meet like this."

She nodded. Then she smiled. She had even, pretty teeth.

Pete gave a half-smile. He shrugged his shoulders and said, "I don't know what to say."

"I should thank you," the girl offered.

Their eyes met. She had large, dark eyes. Pete thought of the eyes of a cottontail rabbit, which always seemed pretty to him. He felt it was safe to look at the rest of her, quickly, so he swept his glance to the ground and then at the two dead men. "It's too bad it had to go that way for them," he said, "but each of 'em had a choice."

He shook his head at the thought of what the men had tried. It was ugly. Then he looked at a spot at the edge of the clearing, beyond the two men, where he saw nothing in particular. He was remembering the last girl he had been with. It had been in Laramie, just before he came up this way.

Her name was Angel, and he had been with her before. She was a soft, smiling girl with blonde hair and blue eyes, ribbon and lace. Her hand was warm but not damp as she led Pete from the dance hall to the room. In the low light of the candle the dress fell away, leaving black lace garters and the satin grey triangle of underpants. As Pete undressed, she unhooked and took off her silk stockings and draped them over the back of the chair that held her dress. She let Pete take off the smaller things, and then she took him into the golden mystery with her hands at the back of his waist, her heels on his calves, her soft voice at his ear. It was as nice as things could be in a dark room with a half-hour limit. The satisfaction had spread through him and stayed with him as he rode to the high country.

He looked at the dead men again and shook his head. This was a bad way to go about it. Who could want to have it that way with a woman, when it could be so pretty? Pete looked at the first man he had shot. The face was expressionless, but Pete remembered the sick look that had been there before the interruption.

"It didn't have to be this way," he said. Even as he spoke he realized he meant two things—

what the men had done, and what it had come to.

"No," the dark girl answered. "They were wrong."

Pete looked at her. She had a simple and honest look to her as she stood there in the blue dress and black, flat-heeled shoes. He remembered the second man saying she was "just a" something, which he never finished. Pete wondered if he meant crib girl or Mexican. Or both. Pete chose to think he just meant her race. Then he asked her, "Do you know either of their names? Do you know who they were?"

"This one," she said, pointing with her left hand at the one who had gone down first, "they called him Tucker. I don't know about the other two."

Pete flinched. "The other *two*?"

"Yes, this one," she said, pointing down again, "and there was another." She raised her right hand and pointed to the place where Pete had heard the commotion. "He was holding the horses," she said.

Pete nodded. Whoever it was, he would know the girl could recognize him if she saw him again. He had probably also gotten a good look at Pete. That made the man doubly dangerous. Pete drew out his pistol, and as he reloaded it, pointing the barrel away from the girl, he looked up and over at her. "Just three, though?"

She nodded.

"I doubt that he'll be back for a while." Pete

checked to see that the empty chamber was in place under the hammer. Then he looked at the girl again and asked, "How did you end up out here with these fellows in the first place?"

"They took me here." She seemed unwilling to say any more.

"Uh-huh." Pete paused. "I don't want to get personal, but if I know a little bit about what's going on, I can help you out of this."

The girl winced, then nodded and smiled, showing her clean white teeth again.

Pete smiled back. She was all right.

She glanced again at the two dead men, and her face tightened in a grimace.

"Let's move away from here," Pete offered. "I need to check on my horse anyway."

She nodded, and he led the way back to the place where he had tied Star. The dark horse whickered low, and Pete made a clicking noise from the corner of his mouth. He patted the horse on the neck, untied him, knuckled the white star on his forehead, and led him over to the girl.

Her face was relaxed in a soft smile.

"Rub your hand on his nose. He already smells you, but that'll help. Now, step closer and pat him on the neck. There you go. He's a good horse. He knows you now. So if anything happens, you can ride him out of here." Pete looked her in the eyes and she nodded back. Then he looked down at the reins in his hands and said, "I need to think about what to do with those two we just left. Why don't you go ahead and tell me what you can, and we'll see what looks like the best thing to do. Start with your name again, if you don't mind."

She pushed her hair back over her shoulder. "My name is Rosa María Peña. I come from Las Cruces, in New Mexico Territory. I came up here to Cheyenne, to go to work as a housekeeper."

"For a family?"

She nodded. "For a man named Elwoot Burr."

"Elwood?"

"Yes, Elwoot Burr. He wrote me by mail that he had a big ranch and he wanted someone to help his wife."

Pete shook his head. "Never heard of him. But go on."

"He met me in Cheyenne, and then we took the train to Laramie. We stayed in a hotel."

Pete kept his eyebrows from raising.

"He gave me my own room. He was very nice. Then this morning we left in his wagon. I was feeling sick"—she laid her hand on her lower stomach—"and I was resting in the wagon, on blankets, when the three men stopped Mr. Burr."

"They didn't see you at that point?"

"Not yet. They wanted to argue with him. I tried not to listen until I heard them tell him to step down from the wagon. Then they told Tucker to hold the horses. That's how I knew his name. I could tell that something bad was going to happen, but I was so scared, I couldn't move there in the box."

"You didn't catch what they were saying?"

"Not until Mr. Burr got down from the wagon, when I knew it was going to be bad. Mr. Burr said something about the King, and one of the other men said, 'When you work for the King, you do things his way.' Then they shot him. And they found me."

"And took you here?"

She nodded. "I think they wanted to go that way, later." She pointed south.

"Colorado." Pete bit his lower lip. "What did they do with the wagon?"

"They left it there next to him. They just left everything. Except the horses. They took the horses."

"And you."

"Well, yes."

"Did you ride in a regular saddle with that dress?"

She nodded.

No wonder they got big ideas, Pete thought. "Well," he said, "what's done is done. I don't want to go to the law with this any sooner than we have to. I imagine someone'll find your boss before long. Did you have a suitcase or trunk?"

"Oh, I forgot to tell you that. I had a valise. The other man took it."

"The one that got away?"

"Yes."

"Does he still have it?"

"No, he just looked in it, put his hands inside and felt around. Then he closed it up and threw it in a canyon."

Pete nodded once, twice. "I doubt he'll take any of this to the law. If he does, I'll be glad to talk to the sheriff. But I doubt he will. I expect he'll come back to look after these two, so we can leave them as they are."

"And where do we go?"

Pete took out the makings and rolled a cigarette as he talked. "I think we'd best make ourselves scarce until we find out who we're up against. We need to find out who the third man is, and who the King is. They'd probably like to get their hands on both of us. I think maybe we should hide out for a while, and I can ask around to see what I can turn up." He licked the cigarette, sealed it, and put it in his mouth.

"You want me to go with you?"

He lit the cigarette. "You're welcome to, but you don't have to."

She looked at the ground and then up at him. "All right."

Pete patted her on the head. "Don't worry, little sister. I'll take care of you."

Chapter Two

The girl turned out to be a good scrapper. She didn't complain about anything, and she was handy around camp. Pete set their camp in the rimrock, where they had a good chance of seeing and hearing anyone who came near. The campsite was under a huge rock overhang, which sloped down and back to form a shelter. As long as they built fires during daylight, they would be all right. Pete built up a low rock wall to screen the flames, and any smoke would be spread out by the overhang rather than rise in a single column.

It was necessary to go a ways for firewood, which they did, dragging back three large cedar branches. Rosy, as she called herself, went about breaking twigs and branches, keeping them in a neat pile, and tending the fire. Pete took the horse to water and brought back a full canteen when he returned to camp.

He knelt in the shade at the edge of the campsite, his right knee on the ground and his right heel under his butt. This Rosy was a good girl, but she still seemed a touch foreign to him. She pronounced her name with a hard *s*, just as she pronounced the word "lazy" as if it were "lacy." She was also heavy on the *r*'s, especially at the beginning of her own name, which she had had to say a few times for Pete. When she pronounced a final *d*, as in "good," "bad," or "Elwood," it sounded almost like a *t*, as Pete had noticed earlier. And the *t* sound, as in his own name, came out sharp and clear. When he went for water, he practiced making the thinner-sounding *t*. The tip of the tongue had to hit the roof of the mouth differently.

Nevertheless, she spoke perfect English, and it wasn't just her speech that made her seem foreign. Pete allowed to himself that it had to do with her color. He knew she was a person, just like Angel or any other woman he had known, but something in her color made her seem like a different kind of person. As Pete watched her move around camp, her dark eyes scanning the country out and away from their hideout, he realized he saw her as something different from his own kind. Not so different as a jackrabbit from a cottontail, maybe, because they couldn't interbreed, but different all the same. He realized that he had always seen his own kind, white people who talked his lingo, as being his definition as people. Then the rest— Indians, Mexicans, Chinamen, and blacks— they seemed to be outside the circle, like they were incomplete or something like that. He hadn't recognized that attitude in himself before, but he had sensed it in the two men he'd left dead down in the timber. Of course there was the he-she stuff boiling in them, too, and that was what did it for them.

He looked at Rosy and nodded. She was a woman all right, but if it came right down to it, he'd take Angel. Or someone like her. That was the picture that came to mind when the boys talked about the golden gate. Suddenly he laughed, quieter than a hiccup. He was remembering a Mexican cowhand who had joked about the *delta negra*. He nodded to himself. He'd bet it was real, but he'd still take Angel.

Rosy looked at him as if he'd cleared his throat.

"Nothing," he said.

She smiled and went back to breaking twigs, and he took out the makings to roll a cigarette where he crouched.

Before sundown they cooked and ate half the bacon he had bought in Laramie. Then they wiped his one tin plate, boiled coffee in a can, and shared the brew back and forth as the sun went down behind them. The dead men seemed to be getting farther away.

The shadows lengthened and then went away. A half-moon was up, and the coyotes started yapping.

"Coyotes," he said.

Rosy turned to him in the moonlight. "They won't come near, will they?"

"Nah. They stay away from people."

The two of them sat in the darkness, and though he couldn't see her very well, he sensed that she had something to say. "Talk," he said. "Say something."

"You have a funny way of talking."

"Oh, I do, do I? What did I say that was funny?"

"You call them *ca-oats*."

"Well, what are they? There's wolves in this country, but that's not them."

"*Co-yo-te*," she said, in three round syllables.

"*Ky-o-ti*, *ky-oat*, all the same. Little yella dog. Hard to kill."

"It's an Indian word."

"I figured that."

"It's the Indians in Mexico. So it's a Spanish word, too. Like *zopilote*, the buzzard."

"Again?"

"*Zopilote.*"

"So-pee-lo-tay?"

"Uh-huh."

"I'll be damned. I bet I heard that before."

"And *guajolote*, the turkey, and *tecolote*, the owl."

"I think I heard the owl word before."

"They're pretty words, aren't they?"

"Yeah, I guess so. But I imagine I'll still say *ca-oat*." He opened his mouth as he pronounced it. Then, hoping she'd catch the tease, he said, "You don't mind?"

"Oh, no," she answered. "It's the way you are."

Pete thought, you lose a little somethin' when you can't see the person you're teasing.

Not long after that, they turned in for the night. Pete had already laid out his bedroll for her and his saddle blanket for himself. The nights would be getting colder, especially this high up. If they were out like this for very long, it would just be a matter of common sense to roll in together. He thought of what she had said about the boss in Laramie. She was a good girl. It was even interesting to think of her being in his bedroll at the moment. He felt a little surge. It sure would be different if that was Angel.

In the morning, after a breakfast of coffee and cold biscuits, Pete told Rosy he was going to leave her in camp by herself for a while. She didn't seem worried.

"I know a fella who lives not too far from here," he said. "He trades horses and sees a lot of people come and go, and he's usually got his ear to the ground. I might be able to learn something from him."

"That's fine," she said.

She remained seated by the fire when he got

up. He patted her on the head and went off to saddle the horse.

Pete rode down from the rimrock in the general direction of Laramie and then veered southeast when he came to the foot of the mountains. After about an hour's riding he was on the ranch of the man he had in mind.

The horse trader's name was Pearl. Pete had known him for over three years. Pearl ran a hardscrabble horse ranch he called the Flat Rock Ranch. His spread was rough and rocky, but he didn't need to run as many head as a cattleman did, so he made out all right. He had a band of brood mares, which he left out to pasture. In addition to raising colts and trading horses, he broke and trained horses for other people. Pete knew he picked up quite a bit of information that way.

Pearl's place pretty well fit the idea of a boar's nest. Pearl was widowed from an earlier time and place, and now he shared his cabin with a couple of hands. From time to time there would also be a hanger-on or passer-through who put up there for a while. Whenever Pete had been inside the cabin, it had smelled of unwashed men, stale smoke, dirty dishes, and bacon grease, along with the horsey smell of all the gear they kept hanging and lying around inside. Outside, he had learned that when he talked to one of the hands, he sometimes needed to keep a distance or stand upwind.

Before he got to the actual headquarters he

heard the sound of a hammer, and it sounded as if someone was driving big nails through thick lumber. As he rode down the slope to the cluster of buildings, he saw two men working on a small circular corral. It looked like Flint and Clell.

As he drew closer, Pete saw that they were indeed Flint and Clell, young buck and old stag. The two bickered whenever Pete was around, and he supposed they argued for the benefit of strangers, for it was evident that they worked well together and got along fine. Right now, Flint was braced against a corral post, and Clell was driving spikes with heavy hammer blows. They let up as Pete came near.

Pete could see that they were building a riding pen. It looked like it would be a little over thirty feet across. There were twelve heavy posts set in a circle, about eight feet apart. The planks were laid jack-over-jill on the ends, apparently for better strength, rather than butt-end against one another on each post. They were rough sawmill planks with few of the ends square, so the method of overlapping them above and below rather than having a continuous band or railing also did away with the need for cutting the plank ends square. The two men were on the sixth course, and it looked as if it was shaping up to be a stout corral.

The three men called out greetings back and forth, and Pete swung down from the saddle. He shook hands with Flint, which he might not have done if it was just the young man. But he always felt it his duty to shake with Clell, so he went through the motions with Flint as well. Today, since Clell was inside the corral and leaning on the top plank, it was as if Pete had to go through Flint to get to the older man.

Pete looked at Flint as they shook hands and exchanged how-are-you's. Pete saw again the straight brown hair, bristly mustache, and week-old stubble. His eyes met the brown eyes that looked like weak coffee. Pete tried not to breathe deeply because Flint always carried the odor of a young man who worked hard and bathed seldom. Flint was tall and lean; he dressed in loose, dirty clothes and had a low-class look about him. But that wasn't why Pete didn't care for him, although his looks and his smell didn't help. What irritated Pete was the constant spouting off. The young man was illiterate and ignorant, but rather than keep his mouth shut and store up what he heard, he was forever speaking up to show his knowledge of the world.

"Nice weather for this kind of work," Pete said.

"Yeah, but just wait. Gonna be an early winter."

"Is that right?"

"Yeah, you can tell."

Pete finished the handshake, noticed a fleck of cigarette paper stuck to the young man's lower lip, and moved away.

Flint turned to the corral post where he had left his hat, presumably so it wouldn't get crushed as he shouldered up against the posts. He put the hat on his head, and Pete saw that it was the same hat as always—a plain brown hat with a pinched crown and a brim that curled up on the sides. It seemed as if he was putting on the hat because Pete was there.

Pete walked over to Clell and shook his hand. Clell was an old man who looked like he had one foot in the grave. It always seemed proper to Pete that he should shake Clell's hand, so he would know he had paid his respects in case the old man cashed in his chips. Clell promoted the idea that he didn't have long to go, and he often said he didn't think he would make it back to Missouri to die. In Pete's view, maybe the old man didn't want to leave, and maybe he just liked to complain.

Clell was not a grand old man. He was just old. He had watery blue eyes and blotchy pale skin that showed liver spots through the thin hair on his temples and on up to his hat brim. His hair was gone all white, with the yellowish tint of a cue ball—or maybe a billy goat's beard, but not for the same reason. He was toothless, and his large nose seemed almost to touch his chin. Today he had several days' worth of white stubble, and the left corner of his mouth was wet where he sucked on the soggy end of a cigarette. He had the sour smell of an old man who didn't bathe and who leaked in his pants. But Pete shook his hand and smiled.

"How are you, Clell?"

"No damn good." The old man stretched out his arm, then opened and closed his fist.

"Looks like a tough job."

"We switch off. But then I don't like gettin' the piss pounded out of me, either." Clell took off his hat and wiped his forehead with his sleeve. He was bald on top, and Pete could see where the brown spots went above the wrinkles on his forehead. Clell put the hat back on. It was an old hat that might have been white or cream-colored at one time but was now weathered grey like old canvas. It had years of sweat stains around the band, and there was a hole worn on the ridge of the crown. Pete had heard him declare, at least two years earlier, that it was his last hat, that an old man like him didn't have any business buying more than a pound of coffee at one time, much less a new hat.

Pete surveyed the inside of the corral. "She looks pretty sturdy."

Clell had picked up his hammer again, and he smacked the post at his side. "You bet it is. This sonofabitch'll be here long after I'm gone."

That was the way it was with Clell. Every topic was likely to come back to the same point. Pete widened his mouth and relaxed it. Then he said, "Where'd you boys hide Pearl?"

"He ain't here," said Flint.

Clell said, "He'll be back in about an hour."

"I guess I could wait."

"You don't have to be a little sparrow fart about it," Clell said. "You could take your turn and hammer a round while you waited."

"I guess I could." Pete looked around for a place to tie his horse, and at that moment he saw Pearl walking towards him from the cabin. Flint and Clell started laughing. Pete shook his head and said, "Clell, I hope you don't die. I don't know what Flint would do. He'd probably die, too, like those Siamese twins."

Clell glanced at Flint, who gave him back a blank look. "Chang and Eng," said the old man. "They chopped wood together."

Pete laughed and shook his head again. It was true that these two were a pair. Among their compatibilities, Clell was Flint's almanac and reading glasses. "I'll see you fellas later," Pete said. "Good talkin' to you." Then he turned and walked towards Pearl.

A man would know Pearl a mile away, by his walk. It was the uneven and bowlegged walk of a man who had spent a great deal of his life on horseback and some of it getting bucked off. Pete had heard him tell more than once that he had walked from Illinois to Oregon when his family moved west. Pearl was a shade over fifty now. He said he had done enough walking when he was ten years old to last him the rest of his life. But in the time that Pete had known him, it seemed that Pearl spent progressively less time riding and more time tending to the other operations of his place. That kept him down on his feet.

Pearl waved and smiled, and Pete returned the greeting. As they came closer to one another, Pearl said, "Hello, Pete. All done with roundup?"

"Yep. Didn't last too long."

Pearl shook his head. "It'll come back."

"Oh, yeah."

They shook hands.

"You look like you're doin' fine, Pearl."

The older man pushed back his hat, a dove-grey hat with a flat crown and broad brim. He had a full head of grey hair as well as a thick grey beard, which he kept trimmed back to about an inch or so. "You know me," he said. "Eat good, sleep good, and feel good." His light blue eyes sparkled. Pearl had fair skin that didn't darken much even when it tanned, and it carried the flush of good health on his cheeks. He clapped Pete on the shoulder and smiled. "Well, are you here to sell something, or is this a social call?"

Pete felt his own spirits rising. For all he knew, the three men who had died yesterday were being worked on by magpies, and he had felt a cloud of gloom over him. He had come to the right place. "I guess it's a social call." Pete glanced at Flint and Clell, who were putting the next plank in place.

Pearl said, "Well, let's go have a cup of coffee

and a smoke, then." He turned and headed them back towards the cabin.

Pete tied his horse to the rail outside and walked into the cabin. He pulled a chair over to sit by the doorway, close to the fresh air and morning sun. Pearl moved around in the darker interior, stoking the fire and rustling up the coffee. Pete watched him clap the lid on the coffeepot and set the pot on the cast-iron stove.

"Be a little while," said Pearl. He picked up a chair and carried it to the doorway, where he could sit in the sunlight with his visitor. He sat down and dipped into his shirt pocket for his tobacco and papers, and Pete did the same. When they had their cigarettes built, Pearl struck a match, lit both smokes, shook out the match, and tossed it outside. He spit out a grain of tobacco as he exhaled the first drag of his cigarette, and he looked at Pete. "Well, it seems like you have a story to tell."

"I sure do. I guess maybe I'll start with a question. What do you know about a man named Elwood Burr?"

"Elwood Burr? Oh, he's a small-time horse trader, runs a few cattle. Why?"

"My understanding is that he got killed yesterday."

Pearl looked at the ash on his cigarette.

It seemed to Pete as if the older man had more to say but was waiting to say it, so Pete went on. "He had a girl with him, a housekeeper he'd hired to help his wife on their ranch."

Pearl raised his eyebrows. "Have you met this girl?"

Pete nodded. "That's who I got the story from. She said he hired her through the mail and arranged to meet her in Cheyenne, then brought her back to Laramie."

Pearl's eyes rolled upward and then down. "From what I know of Burr, which I admit isn't much, he doesn't have—or didn't have—much of a ranch. Less than I do. And I never knew of any wife. Sounds to me like he mail-ordered himself a mistress."

"Or wanted to turn it into that."

"Well, yeah. Does she seem like a nice girl?"

"Seems like. She's not your typical hurdy-gurdy." An image of Angel, blonde and bright, flashed through Pete's mind. As before, it made a contrast with the dark-featured Rosy.

Pearl turned down the corners of his mouth and nodded. "Well, what happened to him?"

"As the story goes, this girl was sleeping, or at least lying down, in the back of his wagon when three men held him up somewhere this side of Laramie."

"Held him up?"

"Stopped him. Made him get out. Then they shot him."

"Any idea why?"

"The girl said she heard them talking about someone called the King. They told Burr that when you're working for the King, you do things his way. Then they plugged him."

Pearl gave a low whistle.

"Do you know anything about any of this?"

"Some. But go ahead and tell me the rest, and then I'll fill you in on what I know."

"Well, these three hardcases just left Burr and the wagon right there. They took the girl and the horses. And her traveling bag, which they threw away later."

"Where'd you come across 'em?"

"Just above Mineral Creek."

"They hauled her quite a little ways. I don't suppose they were up to any good."

"They sure weren't. The one jasper was just pullin' out his lizard when I shot him."

Pearl flinched. "Really. And there was three of 'em?"

"I only saw two. The third one was back in the brush with the horses, and he got away before I could get a look at him. But I would guess he saw me."

"The dirty bastards. What did you do with the middle one?"

"The second one? I told him to pull up his partner's pants, and he came around with the fella's gun. That was my mistake. I hadn't kept track of it. But when he came up with that hog leg, I let him have it."

"You damn right." Pearl took a long drag on his cigarette. "You did right, Pete. You can't let these sons of bitches run all over us."

"I didn't like the business with the girl. That's what brought me into it."

"And it doesn't matter what kind of girl she is. These sons of bitches think they can do anything they want. They steal horses and put a bullet through anyone that crosses 'em. And then they think they can drag some girl out and have their way with her. By God, that's two of 'em down." Pearl took another drag and pinched out the stub of his cigarette. "What's this girl's name?"

"Rosy. Short for Rosa María. Mexican girl."

"They're good, too." Pearl seemed to reflect for a moment. Then he brightened up and said, "You gonna slap your brand on her?"

"I don't know that she's my type." Pete grinned. He wouldn't have jumped to that idea nearly as quick as Pearl did. "But she's a nice girl."

Pearl flicked tobacco off the front of his shirt. "They're all good," he said. He paused and then went on. "You know I had me an Indian wife for a while."

Pete nodded. He knew that the woman had died.

Pearl widened his eyes and pursed his mouth, then relaxed. "Sometimes I think of goin' back to the Wind River country and see about gettin' another." He sniffed. "But enough. Let's get back to your story. Where is this girl?"

"I've got her stashed away up in the rimrock. Thought I'd come see you and find out what I could."

"Well, there's not much more that I know.

This fella Burr, he was a small-timer. Horses came and went through his place. I wouldn't be surprised if he was mixed up with this stolen horse ring and got in somebody's way."

"You mean the King?"

"I don't know who the King is, but that's a name you hear. You hear the name Grant, too, but you never meet anyone that goes with either of them names. I think they're the same man, though."

"How about Tucker?"

Pearl frowned and looked at his nose. "No, I can't say I know anyone named Tucker. Is he one of 'em?"

"The first one I shot yesterday. That was the only name I got."

"Hmmh."

"But you don't know anything about a man called the King."

Pearl shook his head. "I try not to know anything I shouldn't. You know, I try to run a clean place here. I won't touch a horse if I think there's something crooked. You know that."

"Oh, yeah." Pete crushed his cigarette butt on the door sill and brushed the mess outside.

"There's men come and go through here all the time, and I hear all kinds of talk. Lately there's been talk of a stolen horse ring, horses bein' taken down to Colorado and beyond. You can bet that if someone talks about it, he ain't part of it. So everything you hear is chin music."

"I figured as much. But I know more now

than I did before. Or less, maybe. I've got a man with no name and no face, and a man with two names and no face."

Pearl let out a long, slow breath. "It's the hell of it," he said. "You hear all about how this Territory is gonna be a state in another couple years, and how the law will move in on things like this." He spit through the doorway. "But there's always crooks. If we get more civilized, the crooks'll just get better."

"I believe it."

"Let me go check on that coffee," Pearl said, getting up from his chair.

At that moment, a little black goat stuck his head in the doorway.

"Well, look who's here," said Pearl. "Look out for your tobacco, Pete. This little outlaw's the worst thief of all." As Pearl went to move away, the little goat put his front feet on the door sill. Pearl turned around. "Get out!" he said, shooing the goat with his hands. "You've got no business in here. Give him a little kick, there, Pete."

Pete raised his leg and pecked at the goat with the toe of his boot. "Go on," he said. "You don't belong in here."

Pearl came back and sat down. He took a bone-handled jackknife out of his pants pocket and began cleaning his fingernails. "Coffee'll be a few more minutes yet."

Chapter Three

When Pete left the Flat Rock, he waved good-bye to Flint and Clell. By now they had traded places. Clell was shouldered up against a post with his hat tipped to one side, while Flint was inside the enclosure, taking fierce swings with the hammer.

Pete thought of going to the Saddleback, where he had worked for the last three seasons. He was off the payroll, but he had left some of his gear in the bunkhouse and was welcome to stay there as he pleased. In a short visit he might pick up some scrap of information. It would be nearly a two-hour ride north along the foot of the mountains, and then it would be another two hours back up to camp. The three places made a triangle, with camp roughly due west of the halfway point between the two ranches. Pete looked at the sun. It was past mid-morning now. A full trip would put him back to camp sometime in the afternoon at the earliest. That was too long to leave the girl and not check on her. He could go to the Saddleback tomorrow.

He decided to go back to camp but less directly than the way he had come. He would follow the foothills north for an hour, and then he would cut west to the higher country. That was a good idea.

It was a pleasant day, much like the day before. The sun was warm but not hot, and here on the plains, time seemed to stand still. It was the type of day that didn't seem urgent. It seemed as if this day had no stronger purpose than to resemble the day before and the day after as closely as possible. Pete did not sense the fragile quality that had been in the air in the higher country. Here on the plains the sun was shining in the friendly manner of Indian summer, the old impostor.

Star had been moving at a fast walk. There was no need to push the horse, especially with the uphill work still ahead. The light gait of the horse and the broad warmth of the sun combined to maintain Pete's good spirits after the visit with Pearl. He was not actually happy, not as he had been the day before in the afterglow of having had his wick trimmed; but he felt better than a man might after killing two men and giving a third one a reason to be after him. He touched his pistol out of habit, turned to scan his backtrail, and relaxed again as the horse carried him onward.

Pete thought he was nearing the spot where the trail made a "Y." One leg went northeast around a butte and then straightened out north again towards the Saddleback. The other leg went northwest and then angled off west towards the high country. Pete intended to follow that trail, then cut back south to reach his camp.

When he was about a half mile from the place where the road forked, Pete saw a horse and rider come out from behind the butte on the northeast side and turn on to the trail towards him. The horse was barely moving. Pete guessed that the rider intended to meet him at the "Y," and since he would do no good by turning off the trail now, he rode on as he had been doing.

When Pete was within a hundred yards of the spot where the stranger waited, the other man raised a hand in greeting. Pete returned the signal. As he rode closer, he gathered impressions of the man.

The stranger was on a bay horse, a glossy, well-muscled animal. The man's outfit was single-rigged and had a breast collar, and he carried a rope in the usual place. He was dressed in black from hat to bootheel except for a white shirt. The hat was flat-crowned with the brim barely curved on the sides. Drawing closer, Pete saw that the man's frock coat was open but his black cloth vest was buttoned. A watch chain shone in the midday sun. The man's face was in shadow, and he had a beard.

The stranger touched his hat brim as Pete rode up. "Good day," he said.

"Hello." Pete touched his own hat brim in response.

The man smiled. His beard had a neat trim to it, and it looked impressive, dark and sharply etched against the light complexion. His hair, too, was dark and neat, covering half the ear and touching the collar. The man looked to be about ten years older than Pete, which would make him not yet forty. He still had a good build, which was not true of all men who wore that cut of clothes, and he sat well in the saddle.

"Headed north?" he asked.

Pete had already decided to give that impression. "Sure am. Headed for the Saddleback Ranch."

"They've come off roundup by now, haven't they?"

"Yes, sir. We got 'em shipped."

The man put both his hands on the saddle horn. The left hand holding the reins went on top, and Pete noticed an oval-shaped black ring. Pete thought it might be onyx. It seemed as if the man gave him time to look at the ring and then meet his eyes again. The stranger had grey eyes. When he smiled like before, Pete saw that he had straight, even teeth.

"Were you lucky?" the man asked.

Pete drew back on impulse and gave the man a narrow look. "How do you mean?"

"Well, I'd guess you've been to town, and you look like the kind of young man that knows the ladies."

"Well, yes, we get along fine."

"Excuse me. I didn't mean to be so personal. It's a failing of mine. I see someone I like, an honest-looking young man like you, and right away I think I know him better than I do. I'm sorry." The slate-grey eyes softened.

"It's all right."

The stranger nudged his horse so that he gave Pete his right side. He held out his hand to shake. "My name's Flagg. Quentin Flagg. I have the Black Diamond Ranch over that way." He motioned eastward with his chin, in the direction of Laramie.

"Mine's Pete Garnett." He nudged Star around and sideways to shake Flagg's hand. The man had an iron handshake, but there was no apparent effort to overpower his new acquaintance. The grip felt firm and assuring, and the man's eyes were friendly. He released Pete with his eyes first, and as Pete lowered his gaze, he saw the coils of rope against Flagg's leg. As the man was still stretched, Pete also saw the bottom of his coat lifted up to expose the tip of a holster. Pete sensed in that instant that the man was as dangerous as a diamond-back rattler. Then their hands released and they drew apart.

"Beautiful day, isn't it?" said Flagg as he settled back into his seat.

"Sure is."

"Enjoy it while we can." Flagg had both hands back on the saddle horn.

"Oh, yeah," Pete said. "You can see it comin', especially higher up." He motioned with his head.

"Is that right?" Flagg turned the grey eyes on him.

Pete made a quick recovery. "Without a doubt. It always starts earlier up there. The last cows we brought down were over on Sheep Mountain, and all the leaves were turnin'. And that was a week ago."

The man nodded. "Maybe it'll be an early winter."

Pete felt a chill run through him. He had heard that line a thousand times, including Flint's declaration just a little earlier, so it wasn't what Flagg said that shivered him. It was the tone of his voice, smooth and flat and deadly. And although Flagg's voice was new to Pete, there was something familiar about the man himself—some ripple of recognition that Pete felt. He heard himself say, "You never know."

Silence hung in the air for a moment until Flagg said, "Going back to the Saddleback, eh?"

"Yes, sir." Pete's hand went to his shirt pocket for tobacco and papers, and he made a gesture of offering a smoke to the stranger.

44

Flagg twitched one nostril and shook his head. Then his face brightened as he said, "Well, I'm going back to my place, too. It's a nice day just to take a little ride like this."

"It sure is."

"Well, good luck to you. If you're ever over east of here, about eight miles as the crow flies, drop in at my place. There's always someone there, and we love company."

"I'll do that." Pete imagined a second triangle, this one between Flagg's place, Pearl's, and the Saddleback.

"So long, then." Flagg adjusted his reins.

"So long. Nice meeting you."

"It's been my pleasure." Flagg said it as if he was used to settling questions in advance.

As Pete held the small cloth tobacco bag in his hand, he watched the man ride away to the east, across the plain where there was no marked trail. Flagg didn't look back, and Pete imagined it would seem like bad manners if he himself showed any suspicion. So he put the tobacco away, hit the trail north, and kept looking straight ahead.

As he rode, Pete felt danger at his back. For all the friendliness and assurance that the man showed, Pete had a strong hunch about still water running deep. And somewhere beneath the surface there had seemed to be a familiarity, as if they had met before.

Star moved on briskly, his gait untroubled on the open ground. Pete knew the horse had a good eye for the trail, avoiding prairie dog hills and badger holes. This was the time of year when snakes lay out on an open road or trail where the earth was warmer, to enjoy the last of this season's sun before they denned up. As a habit, Pete kept an eye on the trail and on the landscape around him, but he knew Star had a good eye for snakes as well, so he gave the horse rein and turned his thoughts back to trying to place the stranger.

The trail dipped down to cross a gully, and the air was cooler in the shadow. Pete shivered and thought of the day before, the look on the first man's face, the noise of horses in the screening foliage.

Star took them back into the spreading sunlight, and a wave of memory washed through Pete. The face of the man he had shot connected with another face, and it wasn't Quentin Flagg's. The earlier face belonged to a man now dead, too.

It had been early June. He remembered the season because he had seen swallows skittering back and forth beneath a bridge as he rode into Denver. He had come down the road from Fort Morgan, which angled into Denver to meet the old north-south trail that ran from Santa Fe to Cheyenne and the east-west trail that came in from Hays, Kansas, and went on out west to Grand Junction. He saw swallow nests in Denver also, in the stable down the street from the

Edwards Hotel. That was how he remembered the time of year.

The hotel clerk was a picture of discretion, with his dark hair slicked down and his collar buttoned up. He had obviously practiced the art of doing his work with as few words as possible. When Pete asked for a room, the thin-necked clerk nodded and turned the register around. He took Pete's silver dollar and still without a word slid the key and its wooden tag across the counter, his first three fingers covering and then uncovering the number 9. Pete thanked him, crossed the lobby beneath a set of elk antlers, and mounted the stairs, his thumb pressing against the wooden tag.

The clerk had practiced either too much or too little, as Pete would learn later, for he should have given him the key to room 6. When Pete opened room 9, he found it occupied.

The two men inside the room had good reason to be surprised. A man with wings of grey hair at his temples was sitting on the bed, pawing through a strongbox. There was money laid out on the bed cover, and the man was holding a watch and chain in his left hand as he dug with his right. Another man was seated on a wooden chair, turned at an angle away from the door. An open trunk lay at his left foot, the lid standing up. A lady's undergarments were draped on the trunk lid, and the man was pulling a letter from an envelope at the moment of Pete's entry. This man seemed engrossed in his work, for there were other opened letters laid out on a chair in front of him. The whole scene filled in for Pete in an instant, and it remained frozen in his memory.

The first man, the one with the silver temples, was quicker to act than his partner was. He dropped the watch and chain back into the metal box and went for his gun, a movement that was made awkward by his sitting on the edge of the bed.

Pete's gun jumped into his hand and fired. The man jerked backward, firing a shot up over Pete's left shoulder. Then he slid off the bed and landed sitting on the floor, his left foot tucked under him, as the tin box tumbled down next to him. Gold and silver coins, the watch and chain, and other assorted jewelry clattered on the wooden floor.

The exchange occurred in a few seconds, but for all the time since then, Pete could remember every detail in the sequence—the surprise and then anger on the man's face, the cramp of his elbow as he pulled his gun, the rising and falling of his arm, the slump of his body as he went to the floor, the spilling of coins and small precious items that belonged to some unknown person.

In that same instant, the other man was up from his chair and headed towards the open window. Pete hesitated, not knowing if he should shoot the man in the back. Then the man was out the window and gone.

After that there was a long moment of trembling silence, followed by the pounding of footsteps coming up the stairs from the lobby. Then there was the sheriff and not long after that the coroner, both asking questions as the clerk stood by and listened. No woman made an appearance, although it was made clear that a woman had checked into the room by herself.

Pete never did go into his own room, even though it was night time and he had been in the town since noon and could use a rest. He had checked his horse and gear into the livery stable, had gone out to frolic on the town, and had rented the room before going for his personal effects. Now, rather than go into room 6, he handed back the key, went to the livery stable, saddled his horse, and rode north towards Wyoming Territory.

Five years. Pete counted back to make sure. Yes, five years. He had tried to put it out of his mind, but if anything, he had just succeeded in covering it up for a while. Now it all came back in the light of what had happened in the last two days. The thing that matched was the two dead men's faces, five years apart. Maybe it was because they were both caught by surprise at a bad moment. He didn't know.

As for the second man that night in the Edwards Hotel, Pete hadn't gotten much of a look at him. He had gotten one quick glance at the man's face before the man on the bed moved for his gun. Could the man reading the letters have been Quentin Flagg? Pete couldn't say. The fugitive hadn't had a beard, and he hadn't been dressed in black—just a patchwork of grey, blue, and brown going out the window, as Pete remembered the scene. Moreover, the intruder would be older than Flagg. As Pete recalled, there was a touch of grey at his temples also, and Flagg's were solid black. The eyes. Pete did not remember seeing the man's eyes.

The more he thought about it, the more he felt sure there was a connection. He knew he had two of the three dead men caught up together, and now he wondered about the two that had gotten away. Had he seen more than he realized yesterday? He had heard it said that if a man came upon a snake in the trail after he had been thinking about it and expecting it, chances were that he had seen some part of the snake moving through the grass but hadn't registered it consciously. It was like a puzzle he had seen when he was a boy. It was captioned, "Can you see the wolf in the thicket?" The closer he studied, the more thicket he saw. But if he saw the picture at an angle from a few feet away, he could see the wolf.

There was one good way to find out if Flagg was the one. He would ask Rosy.

He decided he had ridden far enough north to cover his tracks, so he turned left and headed for the high country. Once into the timbered slopes he doubled back south, then west for a while, and southwest, and back and forth until he came to the camp.

Rosy must have seen him or at least heard him coming, because she was standing in front of their shelter when he rode up. She shaded her eyes with her hand, but he could see her bright smile.

"How did you do?" she asked as he stepped out of the saddle.

"All right, I guess. I'll tell you all about it. But I've got a question first."

She nodded.

"Did that other man yesterday have a beard?" He motioned with his thumb and fingers in front of his jaws.

"The one with the horses?"

"Yeah. That one."

She shook her head. "No. He had a clean face. Like you."

"Hmmh." There was still a wolf in the thicket as far as the third man was concerned. It wasn't Flagg. A man couldn't grow a beard like that in a day. But he could in five years.

Chapter Four

Pearl had given Pete a few supplies to help out with meals, since Pete had been traveling light and now had a second person to think about at grub time. By himself Pete could make a little go a long way, especially if he dropped by a bunkhouse now and then, where the code of the country made all travelers welcome. He was also in the habit of shooting camp meat when he needed it, but now he was reluctant to touch off a shot and draw attention. Pearl had given him a bag of cold biscuits, two cans of peaches, and a pound of coffee. He also twisted up a little paper package of sugar. The evening before, Pete had learned that Rosy liked sugar in her coffee just as he did, so he accepted that small offering from Pearl along with the other supplies.

Afternoon dinner consisted of the rest of Pete's bacon, a few biscuits, and one can of peaches. Now they had two empty cans to make coffee in, which was quite a convenience.

As they cooked and ate their meal, Pete told Rosy about his visit with Pearl and his meeting with Flagg. Pete's description of the owner of the Black Diamond Ranch did not stir any recognition in Rosy, although she listened and apparently sifted the details.

The sketch of Elwood Burr, of course, came closer to home. She winced and did not smile as Pete told what he had heard. At the end of his short account, he said, "So it sounds like he wasn't on the square with you, and he probably wasn't clean in some of his other dealin's."

"It sounds like he just wanted to use me for a while."

"I hate to say it, but that's sure what it sounds like. He probably figured if he could get a workin' girl that far from home, he'd have some leverage on her."

Rosy no longer winced. Her eyes were wide and serious, and she still wasn't smiling. "I might be poor," she said, "but that doesn't mean I will sleep with some pig of a white man just because he had me in a cage."

"I thought you said he was nice."

"He was. But all I saw was a mask. That's

what it seems like now." Then her face softened. "I'm sorry," she said. "The poor man is dead. Even if he was a pig, he didn't deserve that. And he was nice to me, at least. The other two weren't. They treated me like an—" She bit her lip and looked directly at Pete. "Like I was an animal." She pronounced the *s* as a hard *ess*.

Pete shook his head slowly and lightly. "I'm just glad I came along when I did."

Her eyes watered as she, too, shook her head. "With my people, when we are children we learn respect. We are taught to respect people, not laugh at them if they are poor, or blind, or dark like a crow, or white like the belly of a snake. These men had no respect—not for a woman, not for a person."

Pete got up to shake the coffee grounds from the can he had been drinking from. He stood by the girl and looked down on her.

It touched him to see her wet eyelashes, and he said, "I respect you." He patted her on the head and said, "Don't worry. I'll take care of you."

She moved her head aside. "I'm not your little dog," she said. "And I won't be somebody's *putilla*, either."

Peter stood there feeling stupid. He could not see her face, only the top of her head. After a long moment he said, "I didn't mean . . ."

She sniffed and stood up and then looked straight at him. She took a deep breath and blinked her pretty lashes. "I'm sorry. I know you didn't mean it. But you act that way."

"I guess I didn't realize it."

"I know. I trust you. You saved me from those men yesterday. And I appreciate it. I really do. But there was a minute when I felt like a young cow with a rope around my neck, being passed from one white man to another."

"I'm sorry. I want you to trust me."

She smiled. "I do."

He smiled back, and they moved towards each other. He felt her dampness against his chest, her hands on his upper arms, as he put his hands beneath her arms and pressed her to him.

After a moment she drew back and said, "Thank you. I know you're my friend."

The right words came to him. "I respect you," he said. Then he pressed her to him again, not hard, and released her.

She stood back on her own and smiled. "And I respect you," she said, nodding her head.

Pete felt relieved. There had been a little storm, and it seemed as if they had gotten through it. He looked at the ground and said, "I have a question."

"Yes?"

"What was the word you used?"

"Which word? —Oh, that one. It was a bad word. I shouldn't have said it."

"I guess I know what it means, then."

She glanced around. "You know the word *puta*," she said.

He pictured dark-haired women standing in doorways, painted red lips and black lace. "Uh-huh."

"It means the same thing. I shouldn't use those words."

"Just words," he said. "And I asked."

"It doesn't sound so bad in English," she answered, "but they're bad words." When she said the word "bad," it sounded almost like "bat."

"I've got another one," he said, thinking to change the subject.

"Another bad word?"

"No, not at all. How do you say *water*?"

"*Agua.*"

"Oh, I knew that, now that I hear it. Anyway, I'll go get some *agua*."

She smiled and nodded and joined her hands in front of her.

As he left the camp he saw, from the corner of his vision, that she was using the opportunity to leave camp also. It was an unspoken code that had formed between them. If he got up to leave to get water or for some other reason, he usually went in one direction and she went in another.

After he had filled the canteen he sat on his heels at the edge of the stream. Then he set his hat aside and crouched forward to wash his face. He knew that she came to the stream to wash, too. She washed and combed and ate and slept like he did. He realized also that she had a complete woman's body, that it went through the same processes as Angel's or any other woman's. She was all her own person, complete, with her own boundaries or outer layer, as he had come to understand about other people. When he thought about it, another person seemed to have an outer shell, sort of a layer of air, that made that person whole and set him or her apart from the rest of the world. It said, *Everything inside is me, and everything outside isn't.*

That was what was wrong with the two men yesterday. They didn't see it. They thought they could just shove on in. No respect for the boundaries. No respect for what was whole and personal. Even if a man had to pay a woman, which Pete didn't always have to do, there was a level of respect that said, "May I come in?" and that answered, "Yes, for a while."

Pete wondered if Rosy had ever been with a man, and right away he chastised himself. Even that sort of speculation made him feel like an intruder, invading her privacy. Anything she might have done was her own affair. If things developed between them, then there might be a time to know. But until then, he had no business there.

Although the days were getting shorter, there was a stretch of idle time between dinner and sleep. As a matter of caution, they had a fire when they didn't need it for warmth and then had to let it burn down when there would have been comfort in keeping a good blaze going. Pete and Rosy sat by the glowing coals as dusk gathered around the camp.

"How do you say *crow*? Like the bird."

"*Cuervo*."

He tried it a couple of times.

"That's pretty good."

"Then black crow would be *cuervo negra*."

"*Cuervo negro*."

"Not *negra*."

"No, because it's describing *cuervo*."

"Oh."

"*Caballo negro*, black horse. *Vaca negra*, black cow."

"Uh-huh."

"The same with red or anything. *Sombrero rojo*, red hat. *Camisa roja*, red shirt."

"I see. I guess I knew that. I heard *gato negro* before. *Cuervo negro* would be the same."

"That's right."

He hesitated. "What do you call a person that's dark?"

"*Prieta*. Or *prieto*."

"Like Agua Prieta, the town?"

"That's right."

"Do you call 'em that, like when they're around? To their face?"

"Oh, yes. For example, if a mother has one little one that's darker than the others, maybe she calls him *mi prieto*, my little dark one."

"Really?"

"Yes, and if a man loves a dark girl, maybe he

calls her *mi prieta linda*, my pretty dark girl. You hear it in songs, too. We also say *moreno* or *morena* for dark. *Mi morenita*. That's pretty to say, too."

"And it doesn't bother anybody?"

"No. Why should it?"

"Well, I don't know but—well, one person being darker than another."

She smiled. "We're not all the same. Does everybody in your family have the same color of skin?"

Pete thought. "I've got just the one sister, and she's nearly twenty years older than me, but, yeah, I'd guess you'd say we're the same color."

"And your parents?"

"They died when I was young. I came along pretty late for them." He turned his mouth down in thought, then nodded as he recalled the faint picture he had of them. "Yeah, they were about the same."

Rosy tilted her head as she looked at Pete in the dusk. "How about the eyes? Your eyes are blue. I noticed that right away. Does everyone in your family have blue eyes?"

He thought some more. "No, my sister has brown eyes, and I think my father did."

"Then you're not all the same."

"No, but we don't call each other that way." He paused. "Well, I guess you *will* hear a father call his little girl 'blue eyes,' or a fella might call his girlfriend something like that."

"I know you call a man Red if he has red hair."

"That's true."

"And it doesn't bother him?"

"Why should it? It's just the color of his hair." Then he realized what he had said, and he smiled. "You've thought about this, haven't you?"

"Just about calling someone Red. I never thought about *prieto* and *prieta* before."

"Then I suppose we're pretty much the same after all. We're all people."

"Yes." Then after a pause she said, "But I think there's still a difference."

"What's that?"

"My people learn not to treat someone different if they happen to be lighter or darker than us."

"We learn that, too."

"Does everybody?"

"They teach it to us."

"Then why did white people have slaves? That's such an ugly thing."

"I don't know. But they don't any more."

"But they still think that way. I know that."

"Yeah, they do."

"And they treat us like dirt. Not all of them, but enough."

"I know." He knew he had felt that way, too, even up until today, and the knowledge stung. He took a breath and exhaled. "You know, we're brought up to think that people are equal. We're told that, and we learn to say it. But I couldn't vouch that the majority of people really believes it." He was afraid she would ask him how it all applied to him, whether he thought it or just said it. But she didn't ask.

"It's hard, isn't it?" she said.

"It sure is." Then he thought of how it must be for her, far away from her home and family. In a place like Laramie or Cheyenne, just about everyone you met was lily-white. It must be hard to know that they all saw you as less than white. His lips felt dry. He licked them and said, "I suppose you'll want to go back home just as soon as you can get out of here."

"I haven't thought of that."

"You haven't?"

"You can't predict the future."

"You mean you don't know if you'll ever get out of here?"

"We just don't know what God wants."

Pete thought of the crucifix and the white cord, not visible now in the dark. He had a general notion of how all that worked, the church and such, but he didn't know how to answer. Instead, he said, "But don't you miss home? Don't you want to go back?"

"I miss my family, but it was not all good."

"Oh?"

"When my mother was living, I was happy there. But not any more."

"I'm sorry to hear that. Is your father . . ."

"My father is still alive. But being around him is the part that isn't so good."

"Oh. Does he drink?"

"Yes, he has bad drinking. You know, a habit. And if you're a girl and you're not married yet, you live at home, and it's your duty to take care of your father."

"Is that why you left?"

She waited a moment to answer. "In a way. It was terrible to live there. And if I got married, he would be in the wedding."

"To give you away."

"Yes."

"Sounds bad."

"He's my father, and he will always be my father, and I will respect him. But I don't want to live there."

"Then what do you want to do when you get done here?"

"I don't know yet. I barely got here."

He laughed a short, dry laugh that felt like a release. "Isn't that the truth? And no tellin' how things are gonna work out."

On top of everything else, Rosy was a sensible girl. The chilly air was closing in as the fire died away, and when Pete asked her if she had been cold the night before, she said she had been. No wonder, he thought, coming from a warm climate like she did. Then he explained to her that they would both be better off if they slept side by side under the same covers.

"Men do it," he said, "and think nothin' of it. And if we sleep with our clothes on, we'll stay even that much warmer."

"That's fine," she said.

He gave her the saddle blanket to sleep on, and he used his slicker for his own ground sheet. After spreading the bedroll open for their covers, they crawled underneath. She lay on her left side with her back to him.

Pete lay in the same direction, thinking. Somewhere out there, not far away, were one or two men who would like to get their sights on him and their hands on her. There were three men dead. Next to him was a woman who had helped him learn something about respect and recognize that he in his own way had been a pig. These were things to keep him on his guard.

Even though he was aware of all these circumstances, he knew also that he was next to a woman. The night before, he had found it pleasant to imagine her in his bedroll. Now he felt her presence, her woman-ness, next to him. He wanted to touch her, and he sensed that she wouldn't object. He thought of patting her on the shoulder, and then he realized what it might mean to her. But he felt he had to touch her.

He put his hand on her hip. She reached back and he thought she was going to tap or slap his hand, but instead she moved it up to the neutral area of her waist. Then he leaned forward and kissed her on the back of the neck.

Respect. That was what she deserved. She was a real woman, and she deserved to be treated with dignity.

He was proud of himself for a moment. Then he realized that none of it was clean and simple. He respected her as a person because he yearned for her as a woman; because she had his attention, her message about respect and equality made him perk up and listen. He realized it would not have been the same with a man, or an old woman, or an ugly woman. But this was the way it came to him, and if it was his selfish interest that helped him recognize her as a complete person—well, it could be purer, but it wasn't all bad.

He dozed off and came awake again. His hand was still on her waist, rising and falling gently with her even breathing. She felt relaxed beneath his hand. She was all right. She was a good girl. He felt himself slipping back into sleep, and somewhere between the two worlds of sleep and non-sleep he heard himself think, *she's a hundred percent.*

The King

The problem with Neddy is he doesn't think about anybody but Neddy. Got him in trouble. Made it easy to work him.

Should have told him, "Don't wag that thing or papa will take it away from you." Like my mama told me. Could have told him, could have done it. Just cut it off. Could have done it.

It was more fun to put the gun barrel between his eyes. Listen to him beg. Listen to him make promises. Put the barrel between his eyes. Rub his nose with it. Another man standing there. Laughing.

He said he loved her. Damn near old enough to be his mother. She loves these little potlickers. Said he loved her, wanted to make her a princess, keep her young forever with his love. Nothing is ever a lady's fault. No, of course not.

Scratch his nose with a gun barrel and ask him if he means it. Not any more. I thought I meant it when I wrote it. But not any more. Louder. My friend can't hear you. Tell him you don't love her.

Stick the pistol in his teeth and watch him cry. Then the whip. Push the black handle in his face. Kiss the snake, sonny boy. You know, Indians cut off a woman's nose for this. Then shake the whip loose. Screamed till my arm got tired. Scream for my friend here. While I watch.

So much better that way. You can only pull the trigger once. Lasts longer this way. And you can make him live in fear for the rest of his life. So much better. My way.

Chapter Five

Morning was pleasant once again, chilly but sunny as the day broke. Pete got up first to start the fire. By the time Rosy was up, the rock overhang was absorbing the morning rays of the sun, and camp was a cheerful place.

They breakfasted again on coffee and cold biscuits, sitting on the rocks that had come to be their camp stools. Pete felt that the confidence between them was growing. They were just living from one day to the next, and he had no idea where either of them might be in a few days or a week from now. His immediate plan was to get her to a safe place and then to see if any more trouble came his way. In the meanwhile, the mutual confidence was a good feeling.

After a second cup, or can, of coffee he told her he wanted to make another trip to see if he could learn anything more about this business they were caught up in.

"It's a ranch where I used to work. I should be gone about the same length of time I was gone yesterday. Do you think you'll be all right?"

She nodded.

"I think so too. Nobody's come around at all. I'll look around on my way out, and if I see where anyone's been near, I'll come back."

"That's fine."

He thought of kissing her on the cheek, but again he didn't know how she would take it. So he just touched her forearm and then got up to saddle the horse.

After looking over the area surrounding camp and finding no sign, he put Star on a fairly straight line towards the Saddleback. If Flagg was in the habit of riding from the Black Diamond Ranch to the foothills and back, there would be less chance of meeting him this way.

Pete rode through dark timber and aspen groves, sunny meadows and sagebrush flats, working his way diagonally down the mountain. When he was in the sunlight it was warm on his face, but fall was in the air and he did not take off his denim jacket.

About an hour and a half of riding took him to the Saddleback Ridge, a rocky formation on the western edge of the ranch. He came at the ranch from the south side of the Saddleback, switching back and forth down this one last mountainside before coming into the rolling hills and plains.

This was hard country, green and smiling for a few summer months but bitter through the long months of winter. None of this country was easy, not for a thousand miles north, south or west, or for five hundred miles east. Here along the Laramie Plains it could be especially bleak. There was not a cottonwood tree on the whole of the Saddleback range. There were cedars and brushy growth, and some willows along the streams, but none of the tall, friendly trees that grew so commonly along the Platte and along the smaller streams up and down the eastern side of the Territory.

The Saddleback headquarters were down in a protected pocket with a fringe of cedars at the edge. Brush and little trashy trees grew along the watercourse where the original homesteader had staked out his hundred and sixty acres. By now that individual and several others had sold out to a company called the Saddleback Land and Cattle Company. It controlled enough streams and waterholes to hold together a range four miles across and eight miles long. Most of it was free range, but whoever controlled the water controlled the range, so this stretch of country was essentially the Saddleback's, even though it held little of the land by actual deed.

There were few fences except around haystacks and some waterholes, so cattle from various outfits mingled together. That was what roundup was for, to separate and brand according to ownership. Most of the branding was done in the spring when the new calves were with their mothers, and shipping took place in the fall. After the bad winter, roundup had been pretty light.

There was talk now of putting up more hay in the years to come, and fencing more range, and controlling the herds more closely. As Pete saw it, that meant he would spend more time digging postholes, stringing wire, putting up hay in the summer, and forking it out in the winter. But until then, the country was wide open and a fellow's life was, too. It meant that he was laid off in the winter, but that had never bothered him. He had never gone hungry and didn't expect to, not now when he was still a couple of years shy of thirty and still had muscle in his arm.

As Pete rode into the headquarters, there wasn't much activity. The horse herd had been turned out, and the cattle wouldn't be brought in close to headquarters until the harder weather came. Pete knew that the foreman and the cook had gone with the train when they shipped the cattle. The cook would winter in Omaha, and the foreman would be back at his leisure. Of the three remaining hands, two would go home for the winter and one would stay.

The one who would stay was Chicago Thorne. He had been at the ranch a year longer than the others, so he stayed on the payroll through the winter. Pete found him in the bunkhouse, where he was drinking coffee and oiling his saddle leather. The bridle was already taken care of and hanging from the back of a chair.

Chicago Thorne was a man who kept to himself and did his work. He seemed to keep the past under wraps, as no one knew much about him except that he said he came from Chicago and his last name was Thorne. As a general rule in this country, men did not pry into someone's past. They took a man for what he was and could do now. Thorne had a variety of talents. He could cook, and he wielded the long-handled fork and the pot hooks whenever he was needed to do so out on the range, and here at the bunkhouse he baked biscuits and pies in the large cast-iron stove in addition to rustling steak, potatoes, and beans. He must have picked up blacksmithing at some earlier time, as he was handy at repairing wagons and tools. He made branding irons, and he could turn out a running iron in a matter of minutes. In the winter he trapped coyotes, and last winter he had caught a wolf in a jaw trap.

For all his talents, Thorne was a young man, a year or so younger than Pete. He was perhaps an inch shorter than Pete but still in the range of average height. Often when Pete saw him, standing or sitting, he thought of a bullet. That was the general shape of Chicago Thorne's build. He had a round chest and abdomen, not fat, and his shoulders were not broad. They didn't square out from the black leather vest. There was not much contour from the base of his neck to the brim of his hat, which was a charcoal-grey model with a round crown, narrow brim, and rattlesnake hatband. He had short dark hair and a dark mustache that he kept trimmed. His eyebrows grew together, and beneath them was a pair of quick, dark brown eyes.

He looked up from his work as Pete walked into the bunkhouse. "Hello, Pete," he said. "There's coffee."

"Thanks. I believe I'll have some." Pete went to the kitchen and helped himself to a cup. Then he went to the table and sat down across from Thorne.

"What brings you here today, Pete?"

"Thought I'd pick up a couple of things."

"Uh-huh." Thorne had a stirrup fender held out and was rubbing on oil with a soaked sock. "How'd you make out in town?"

"Oh, all right."

"Last time I saw you, it looked like a yellow-haired gal was after your summer wages."

"She's nice enough." Pete sipped his coffee. Thorne's remark irritated him. From time to time the bullet-headed man dropped a remark

71

like the one he just did. It served to remind Pete of the year before, when he had gotten blind drunk after fall roundup. Thorne himself was a careful drinker and was on his guard when he went to town, so he could make comments like that. "I knew her from before," Pete added.

"Uh-huh." Thorne took two long swipes on the stirrup fender.

The bunkhouse door opened, and a tall man walked in. "Hello, Pete." It was Richard De Chevre, also known as Elk Legs.

"Hello, Rich."

"Out and about, are you?" Elk Legs headed for the kitchen as he spoke.

"Yep. How about yourself?"

The answer came from the kitchen. "Goin' home in a couple more days."

Pete nodded to himself. Elk Legs went home each winter to Wisconsin, where he delivered coal. The other hands knew that this year he had a special mission. He had saved enough money for Verna's monument.

Verna had been his sweetheart until she died. That had been two years earlier. Now he carried her locket. Pete imagined it had her picture as well as a lock of her hair, but he had never seen the little gold case opened. Elk Legs carried it on a chain like other men carried a watch. Her parents had given her a headstone, and Elk Legs had gotten their permission to have a marble pedestal placed beneath it. He told the other hands that he had the words for an inscription all worked out, but he never said what they were. Pete was sure they would be melancholy.

Elk Legs walked back into the main room. He was tall and lanky, and with any but a tall horse it seemed as if he stepped into a stirrup like shorter men would push down on a shovel. He had long, straight, dark hair, and a narrow head with close-set, dark blue eyes and a pointed chin. He stayed clean-shaven and had a light complexion, and he usually carried a sad air about him.

Elk Legs sat at the end of the table. He was wearing his white, pointed-crown hat with the black horsehair hatband, and he rested his chin on his left palm as he leaned forward on the table. He didn't pay any attention to what Thorne was doing.

Pete recalled a discussion that Elk Legs and Thorne had once had. The long-legged puncher had recommended using powder, either corn starch or a talc, to take the squeak out of a saddle. Set the saddle upside down and powder all the cracks real good, he had said. Thorne said he'd try it some day, but he never did anything more than clean and oil the saddle, which he did nearly once a month.

"What do you fellas know about Elwood Burr?" Pete asked.

Elk Legs shook his head in the negative.

Chicago Thorne, who was seated sideways to Pete, raised his eyebrows but did not look around. "Two-bit horse trader," he said. "About like your friend Pearl, maybe a grade lower." He lifted the stirrup fender and looked at the rough leather on the underside. "Why?"

"Oh, Pearl mentioned him."

"Not surprised," said Thorne, turning the saddle around.

Pete took out the makings to roll a cigarette. He did not offer the tobacco around, because Elk Legs did not smoke or drink and Thorne smoked his own tailor-mades. He kept them in a tin can and smoked only in the bunkhouse or outside it, never on the range. Pete rolled his smoke. After he lit it he said, "Was over at Pearl's yesterday. He said there's been a little trouble with stolen horses."

"Is that so?" Thorne reached into the left pocket of his vest and drew out a small, narrow-bladed clasp knife which he often used to clean his fingernails. Now he opened it and scraped at a caked substance on the back of the saddle. "Did Pearl say what's-his-name was in on it?"

"No, not really. But his name came up, and I was curious."

Thorne put the knife away. "Where you stayin', Pete? Or did you come back here for a while?"

Pete took a puff on his cigarette and said, "Up on the mountain."

Thorne still didn't look at him. "Must get cold up there."

Pete smiled to himself. "Not so bad yet."

Chicago Thorne turned from his work to take

a sip of his coffee. He gave a half-smile. "If it gets too cold, you know you can stay here any time."

"Oh, I know. And thanks. I probably will."

Thorne dipped the sock into the open can of oil and daubed it on the saddle skirt.

Pete decided to go at his next question indirectly. "Think it'll be an early winter?"

"No tellin'," said Elk Legs.

Thorne took a deep breath and let it out. "Hard to say."

"Heard it from two different places yesterday." Pete looked at Elk Legs, who just looked back.

Thorne answered, "Oh?"

"Yep. First one was at Pearl's. Heard it from that young fella Flint that works there." Getting no answer, Pete went on. "Second time was after I left Pearl's. I met a man on the trail. He said the same thing."

"Might be something to it," said Thorne.

"Said his name was Flagg. Said he had a place called the Black Diamond Ranch, back towards Laramie."

"I've heard of him," said Elk Legs.

"Have you, Chicago?"

"Just a little. I think he has horses."

Elk Legs said, "That's what I heard, too."

"Do you think he knows Burr?" Pete asked.

"Could be," said Elk Legs.

Thorne rubbed at the leather with his thumbnail. "I bet Pearl could tell you better than we could."

"I bet he could. I didn't think of that because I didn't know that Flagg was in the horse business."

"Then why did you wonder if he knew Burr?"

Careful, Pete thought. "It just now occurred to me when you said he had horses."

"Oh." Thorne turned and took a sip of coffee, glancing at Pete as he did so. Then, looking as if a thought crossed his mind, he turned his chair around and rested both forearms on the table. He folded his lips together and then said, "Hard to say. Flagg's a newcomer. Seems to have money. This fellow Burr is just a little fish."

Pete nodded and tipped his ashes in the shallow can that served as an ash tray.

Elk Legs cleared his throat. The other two looked at him but he said nothing.

Chicago Thorne reached into his trousers pocket and pulled out his nickel-plated watch, which was at the end of a braided leather strap attached to his belt loop. He opened the watch, looked at it without saying anything, and closed it. Then he wound the watch, an action he performed two or three times a day, as Pete had noticed. "Dusty should be back pretty soon," Thorne said. "He went to turn out a few head that we didn't want in this close until later."

Pete took that as the end of the conversation about horse dealers unless he wanted to push it. He smoked his cigarette down and crushed it. Then he tipped up his coffee cup. "I think I'll go through my gear," he said. "Pick up a couple of things I might need."

Thorne nodded and turned back to his work. Elk Legs sat as before, and Pete went to the far corner of the room, where his spare warbag lay under a bunk.

Seated on the bunk, he set the canvas bag on the floor in front of him and opened it. He took out the extra set of spurs and set them at the foot of the bunk to get them out of the way. Then he laid out a wool overshirt, set a pair of pants and a pair of wool gloves on top of it, and rolled the items into a tight bundle. There was not much left in the bag—just a few odds and ends of handkerchiefs, extra socks, long-handled underwear, two lightweight shirts, a curved-stem pipe he never smoked, and a pocket-sized tally book he never wrote in. He put the spurs back into the bag, closed it, and put it under the bunk. Then he went outside without saying anything more to the other two men.

Pete was tying his new bundle onto the back of his saddle when Dusty rode into the yard. The rider waved from a ways off and then rode up next to Pete and dismounted.

Dunstan Travis, or Dusty, was a good-looking young man. He was about twenty-five years old, with a good lean build. He had brown hair and blue eyes, and a full mustache that grew down to the corners of his mouth. He was usually cheerful, and his smile lifted the neat mustache to show his white teeth.

"Howdy, stranger."

"Hello, Dusty."

"Ridin' the grub line?"

"Not exactly. Came to pick up a couple of things."

"When are your sport hunters due in?"

"Not for another ten days." Pete glanced at the bunkhouse. "But I need to let on that I'm gettin' outfitted right now."

"Oh."

Pete knew Dusty was a good cowboy, all the way around. He was good with horses, knew his cattle, and could rope with the best. He could also keep something under his hat. Pete motioned with his head towards the barn, and the two of them walked leading their horses in that direction.

Dusty looked at Pete and smiled. "Looks like you got away from town all right."

Pete laughed. "I did. No harm came to me. Seems like Chicago was worried about me."

"You know him. Never slips."

"And likes to remind people that do."

Dusty looked back and nodded.

When they got to the barn, Pete waited till Dusty unsaddled his horse, rubbed it down, and turned it into the corral. Pete had Star tied to the hitch rack, so he stood next to Dusty as the two of them leaned with forearms on the corral.

Dusty's tan hat was pushed back on his head, and he seemed at ease.

"I don't want to tell you anything you'd just as soon not know," Pete began.

Dusty nodded. "Don't worry. Tell me what you want."

"I'd like to borrow a horse for a few days."

"Now?"

"Uh-huh. I've got a party who's on foot, and I need to get her to town."

Dusty looked at him with a grin. The last time Dusty had seen him had been with Angel.

Pete shook his head. "No, it's not who you think. It's someone else, and the less said at this point, the better."

Dusty brought his upper lip and mustache down over his lower lip and widened his eyes.

Pete went on. "But you might hear something." He motioned with his head toward the bunkhouse. "If you do, and if there's something you think I ought to know, I'd appreciate it."

Dusty nodded. "Sure."

Pete licked his lips. "Do you know anything about a man named Quentin Flagg?"

"I heard he's the owner of that new horse ranch, the Black Diamond. But I haven't met him."

"I have."

"Bad?"

"No tellin'. But before that, I stumbled into what looks like a stolen horse operation. I need to ask Pearl about this fellow Flagg. I've got a feeling that he's in on it somewhere."

Dusty shrugged. "I don't know. I'll be gone in a couple of days and not be back until spring, but I'll keep my ears and eyes open in the meanwhile."

"It could be bad," Pete went on, "and someone might be after me before long. I don't want to weigh you down with all of it now, but if anything happens, Pearl would be the person to talk to."

"And you need another horse for a little while?"

"And a saddle. I should have 'em back in a day or two."

Dusty took a folded handkerchief out of his hind pocket and rubbed it across his forehead. "I could let you have Chub. You know I made a deal to leave him here for the winter. You could bring him back whether I was here or not. I could tell Thorne."

"That would be fine. You know, I need this horse for one of my greenhorns."

"I thought so." Dusty paused. "We can put one of these extra ranch saddles on him."

Pete smiled. "Chicago has one inside that he's getting all oiled up. Maybe I could ask for it."

Dusty laughed. "Sure."

It didn't take long to catch Chub and get him saddled. Pete looked at the sun. "About noon, or maybe a little less."

Dusty, who didn't carry a watch either, glanced up and said, "I'd say so."

They had put the bridle on over the halter so Pete could lead Chub with a lead rope. Dusty knotted the reins and looped them back over the saddle horn. "You're all set," he said.

Pete held out his hand. "Well, so long. I hope to see you in a day or two."

Dusty shook his hand and gave him a smile and a nod. The tan hat was pushed back, not quite as much as before, and the sky-blue eyes were steady. "You bet. And if not then, later."

Pete smiled and nodded, and then in a half-comic impulse, he laid his right forefinger against his cheek and pursed his lips.

Dusty returned the confidence by pulling his hat down level and dropping his left eyelid in a wink.

Chapter Six

As Pete rode away from the Saddleback, he found himself thinking about Chicago Thorne. The man seemed to have plenty locked up in that bullet head—like the cigarettes he had in a tin box, or the metal flask of whiskey he kept in his warbag but never brought out in anybody's company. A man who played solitaire and kept his fingernails clean—that was Thorne. The man who never slipped and who liked to remind others about the times they did.

Pete didn't like it, not the memory or the reminder. It was the one time when he had simply blacked out. It happened a year ago. They came off roundup and went to town—for pissy whiskey and wild, wild women, as they said. That was before he met Angel. He got payday drunk and then some, and he went to the room with a mouse-haired woman named Ruby. That was all he remembered. He woke up the next day in the Trail Hotel across town, flat broke and lonely sick on the residue of liquor. Ruby was nowhere to be found. It was the only time he had ever gotten that drunk, and he wondered if it would happen again. He had been out to cut his wolf loose a few times since then, and it hadn't happened. He wasn't likely to forget it, though, especially when he had Chicago Thorne around to remind him.

Thorne did have one good suggestion all the same, and that was to ask Pearl about Flagg. Pete thought there was enough time to go by that way and still get back to camp without giving Rosy too much cause for worry. Then he decided it would be too conspicuous to lead a saddled horse across all that open country. Better, he thought, to get the horse to camp and then see about a visit to Pearl.

As an additional precaution, he decided not to return to camp by the same route he had taken down to the Saddleback. He would follow the trail toward Pearl's for a couple of miles, then cut into the foothills and follow a broad curve up the mountain.

Pete went on, riding Star and leading Chub. He hadn't told Rosy he was going to try to find her a horse, and he hoped it would work out all right. He didn't know what kind of a rider she was, but Chub was a gentle horse and should give no problem. She could wear the pair of trousers he had picked up, and he had an extra undershirt in his gear back at camp. She could wear that and the wool overshirt, and she should be able to ride comfortably.

By now the day was warm enough that it was worth a stop to take off the jacket. While he was at it, he could water a clump of buffalo grass. He brought the horses to a stop and swung down, then wound the lead rope around his saddle horn. Holding Star's reins, he stood away from the horses and relieved himself. He looked at the sky above him. This was it, he thought. A lot of men would tell you that. It was a good feeling to be able to let 'er go wherever you happened to be, not like in the cities where it all had to be done inside a room or the four narrow walls of a privy.

He took off the jacket and tied it onto the back of the saddle with the bundle of clothes for Rosy. The slicker was back at camp. He looked at the sky again. Thunderstorms didn't blow up so quickly at this time of year. If there came a rain it was more likely to be a slow, cold one. Still, it always seemed that when a fellow left his slicker in the wagon or back at camp, that was when he needed it.

He was pulling tight on the leather thongs when he heard a noise at his back. Glancing over his left shoulder, he saw two riders coming from the east. They were less than a hundred yards away. The one on the left was Flagg.

Star was already looking at the other horses, as was Chub. Pete unwound the lead rope from his saddle horn. Then, trying not to seem in a hurry, he mounted up and waited for the riders to come nearer.

Flagg was on the bay horse again and was dressed as he had been the day before. The other man, who rode at Flagg's left, was riding a sorrel horse with a wide blaze and front socks. The two horses were even in height, and the second man seemed a little taller than the man in black.

The two waved as they came nearer, and Pete waved back. He could hear the clump of the horse hooves on dry ground, then the breathing of the horses, the jingle of the bits, the squeaking of saddle leather.

"Well, it's my young friend on the dark horse," said Flagg. "Hello there."

"Hello."

"Barnett, isn't it?"

"Garnett. Pete Garnett."

"Of course. Garnett, this is Logan Gregory. He works for me."

Pete touched his hat brim, and Gregory did the same. The man had broad, clean features and dark eyes. He wore a wide-brimmed brown hat that closed down over neatly trimmed, wavy brown hair. He was probably in his early thirties—broad-chested and strong-looking, in the prime of his life. In contrast to Flagg he was clean-shaven, and in contrast to a common cowpuncher he did not have a rough, weathered look about him. Beneath a denim jacket he wore a yellow shirt and a black leather vest, with a watch chain like Flagg's. He also wore light brown leather gloves.

"Are you the foreman?" Pete asked.

Gregory smiled without showing his teeth, and then he said in a smooth Texas voice, "You might say I'm the gatekeeper."

"Logan spends most of his time at the ranch," said Flagg. "I don't have a crew of men yet, so he hasn't been pushed up the ladder."

Pete looked at the hired man again. He had a closed-mouth smile, as if there was a pretty good joke going on and he was the only one to understand it. Then Pete noticed he had a dark leather thong that went around his neck and disappeared beneath his shirt. Pete thought about Rosy's crucifix and wondered what the man might have. Probably not a crucifix or religious medal—more likely a ring or some other memento from a girl.

"Lose your partner?" Flagg's voice came at him unexpected.

Pete gave him a frowning, questioning look. He had the feeling that the other two were sharing a joke.

"Empty saddle. Looks like you lost your gal."

Pete burned quick. "Who said I had one?"

"Oh, there I did it again." He clicked with the corner of his mouth. "I was just joking. We joke a lot, don't we, Logan?"

"All the time."

Flagg smiled and his eyes were friendly. "It's just an unusual sight, you know, and I thought it would be ungracious if I just came out and asked what you were doing with that horse."

"I borrowed it from Dusty Travis at the Saddleback. I'm due to take out some sport hunters here in a while."

Flagg gave him a half-wide look. "I didn't mean to seem inquisitive. If you borrowed a horse, that's your business." He smiled again. "It must be a good feeling, to be done with work for the season. Free to come and go, camp out in the open."

"It's nice to be free," said Pete, "but it means bein' off the payroll."

Gregory's voice came out smooth and clear. "There is no rose without its thorn."

Pete looked at him. "That's why I have to pick up more work."

Gregory nodded as if in agreement. "All work is good work," he said.

Flagg spoke up. "Some of the folks you take out here have never been to the wilds before. They miss the comfort of four walls."

"Could happen," Pete said.

"If it does, don't be shy about bringing them to the Black Diamond. It's not a hunting lodge, but it's civilized. Isn't it, Logan?"

"All the comforts."

Pete adjusted his reins and straightened out

the loose ends. Then he said, "Thanks. I'll keep that in mind."

"Well," said Flagg, "we don't want to keep you. It looks like you're on your way somewhere."

Sure, thought Pete. *I could lead you right to my camp.* Then he said, "I'm on my way to the Flat Rock Ranch to visit with old horse trader Pearl."

"I know Pearl," said Flagg. "Good man."

"Uh-huh. I was going to get his advice on this horse. You don't notice it now, but he throws his head a lot. I wonder if I ought to try a different kind of bit."

The Texas voice came out again. "I'd try a hackamore bit. That'll keep his nose down."

Flagg spoke right away. "Pearl's the best one to ask. You don't want a horse that'll throw a parcel of soft goods into the cactus." He smiled the assuring smile.

He knows I have the girl. Probably wants me to give her up the easy way. Pete cleared his throat. "Well, that's where I'm going. You're welcome to ride along if you'd like."

Flagg and Gregory exchanged a glance and then the boss said, "Thanks all the same, but we're meandering. I'm showing Logan the country."

"That's fine," Pete answered, getting his reins and the lead rope straightened out, the reins in his left hand and the rope in his right. He nodded to the two men.

"See you later," said Flagg.

"Good luck hunting," Gregory added.

As Pete rode away with the two men at his back, he was perturbed again. Of all the luck, he had to run into Flagg a second time. He was sure the man meant something with his hints about the partner, the saddle, camping out, and the soft parcel of goods. Flagg must be connected to the horse ring. He probably knew Burr. Whoever the King was, Flagg probably knew him, too. Maybe wanted to hand the girl over to the King. That would be a good favor on the part of a horse breeder who wanted his stock left alone.

Pete looked at the sun. He was going to have to move along. Now he would have to go to Pearl's anyway, and that would put him back in camp later than he wanted. Damn the luck for running into Flagg.

After he had gone about a mile farther, he opened the horses into a trot. Chub kept pace with Star, and they covered a couple of miles in short time. Then Pete slowed them to a walk. He would trot them again after a while and then slow them back down. They would be able to rest awhile at Pearl's, but he didn't want to work them too hard in the meantime. It was a good idea not to have a horse worn out at the end of a ride.

When Pete rode into the Flat Rock there wasn't much going on. Pete figured the men were probably having their midday meal. He looked at the riding pen that had been in the works on his last visit, just the day before. The corral was finished, with a cap rail of planks laid flat around the top. It looked solid, with sides over five feet high. A horse would know he was in there.

Pete rode through the yard and saw a saddled horse tied to a snubbing post. He remembered seeing the same horse, a young sorrel, saddled and tied the day before. He assumed Pearl was getting the young horse used to having a saddle on his back. Later, Pearl would probably tie on a bag of grain to increase the weight. The old horse trader had a whole repertory of methods for breaking horses to the saddle or to harness, and horses that came from him were usually known to be well trained.

Pete called out as he rode up to the cabin. Flint appeared in the doorway, his hat on.

"Yo," he said.

"Hullo, Flint."

"Where'd you smooch the horse?"

"Borrowed it." Pete breathed out heavily as he stepped down from the saddle. If Flint didn't get shot for remarks like that, he'd learn by and by not to make them.

"Well, come on in. We're just finishin' dinner."

Pete tied the horses and stepped into the cabin. He could smell fried meat. It was dark inside, especially after coming in from the bright daylight. As his eyes adjusted he saw

Pearl and Clell sitting at the table. They were wearing their hats and apparently enjoying their after-dinner smoke. Flint had moved back into a darker area of the cabin, where the walls were hung with harness, horse collars, and assorted straps with steel rings and buckles.

Pearl spoke up. "Have a seat, old boy. We just finished eatin', and the boys licked their plates. But I could cook up some more in short order."

It sounded like a good idea, especially with the smell of grub in the air, but Pete decided he'd wait to have a meal with Rosy. "No, thanks, Pearl. I think I'll wait."

"You sure? Nice young antelope. Flint just killed it last night."

"So tender you could cut it with a fork," Clell said. "Even I could eat it."

"No, thanks. But it sounds good." Pete sat at the table, and he could see the plates had been wiped clean. A few biscuit crumbs remained, and that was it.

"Well, then," said Pearl, "I'll be sure to send some along with you."

Pete's eyes were well adjusted to the dim interior by now. He met Pearl's look and nodded. That was good of Pearl, like sending along the sugar. Pete sensed that Pearl hadn't told Flint and Clell about the girl, so he decided to ask him separately about Flagg as he had done with the topic of Elwood Burr.

Flint came out of the dark end of the cabin

and sat at the table next to Pete. The young man smelled as he had the day before.

A motion from across the table caught Pete's attention. He saw Clell looking at Flint. The old man's eyes brightened. Then he smiled, looked at Pete, and said, "Flint don't believe me that Chang and Eng slept four in a bed with their two wives."

"Who?"

"Them Chinese twins. They had it worked out so they could each have at a woman. Had a passel of kids."

"Aw, go on," said Flint.

"Fact. I read it in one of them story papers. I think they was even married to sisters." Clell looked at Pete again. "Young buck thinks I'm makin' fun of him. Just because things have been sort of rock hard for him for a while. Ain't been to town."

"Trouble is," Flint declared, "ain't none of us been gettin' any coony. Then they take it out on me."

That was a new one. Pete recalled that Flint was from Kentucky. He must have brought the word with him.

Clell pulled the wet cigarette from his lips and tipped its ash in the can on the table. "Don't bother me any. My rooster don't crow any more anyway."

"Mine does," Flint said, taking out his tobacco and papers. "He's up early ever' mornin'."

"Well, that's just fine," Clell said, laying the

cigarette back on his lower lip. "But I tell you, they slept four in a bed. Ain't that right, Pete?"

"I don't know a thing about it."

" 'Course, it might do the boy good to go to town anyway." Clell sucked on his cigarette and it glowed. "A little dip in the honey pot would sweeten him up."

Flint looked up from rolling his cigarette and said, "Yeah, whose honey pot?"

Pete thought of Angel or someone like her having to put up with the odor of Flint as he climbed aboard. He wondered if Flint knew enough to clean up before he went to rustle petticoats. Men who lived like this got to where they couldn't smell themselves.

Flint looked back at his cigarette. "Do *you* some good, too."

Flint seemed sullen until Pete realized it was probably a way of talking that Flint and Clell got into when company was around. It happened like that at the Saddleback, too, and if Elk Legs wasn't around when a newcomer dropped in, the others took to talking about women.

"Don't need it," Clell returned. "I can get get drunk right here. Whiskey's been more of a darlin' to me all these years anyway." Clell wrinkled his nose.

Pete looked at the old man and could see the dark area across the bridge of the nose and the upper cheeks. In better light he had seen the little red lines of bloodshot veins, and even in the half-light he could see the flush.

Flint licked his cigarette and lit it. "You two act like I'm the only one that gets hard up."

Pearl blew out a cloud of smoke. "I never said that. If you've heard me say anything, you've heard me say I'd like to get me another woman. Maybe even squeeze her for a pup. I might have to build another cabin, but I could stand to do that." He looked at Pete and grinned. "My pony can still lope. He might be pastured in winter grass, but he can get up and go."

Pete laughed. He knew that Pearl had never had any kids, and he enjoyed the older man's optimism.

"By God," said Flint, "I hope I still got beans when I get to your age."

"You got to get there first," Pearl said, crushing his cigarette.

"It's up to the beggaries of fate," Clell added.

"Sure," said Flint, narrowing his eyes as he drew on the cigarette.

"Pete, you sure you wouldn't like something? Coffee?"

"No, thanks, Pearl. I just dropped by for a minute. I wanted to get your opinion on this horse I borrowed." The line that had worked on Flagg and Gregory was good enough for Flint and Clell.

"You want me to take a look at him right now?"

"When you have time."

"I've got time now."

"Well, all right."

The two of them got up and walked outside, leaving Flint and Clell to work up another topic.

Pearl ran his hand down Chub's front shoulder. "Looks like a good horse. Have any trouble with him?"

"Not really." Pete glanced at the cabin. "I wanted to ask you about something else."

Pearl nodded. "Let's walk 'em around the yard, then."

When they were a ways from the cabin, Pete said, "I met this fellow named Flagg. Do you know him?"

Pearl looked sideways at Pete as they led the horses. "Oh, sure. I've bought a couple of his culls, and I told him I'd break riding horses when he needed me to."

"Have you known him long?"

"No, not really. He hasn't been in the country that long. Maybe six months at the most."

"That's probably why I haven't heard of him. He said he knew you. How about his man Gregory? Do you know anything of him?"

Pearl looked at Pete and shook his head.

"Did Flagg come by here since I was here yesterday?"

"No. Why?"

"Well, I ran into him yesterday after I left here, and then again today. Seems like it might be more than a coincidence."

"Might be."

Pete stopped and turned towards Pearl, who

also stopped. "I think he knows I have the girl."

Pearl's eyes widened. His hat brim was up a ways in front, and he was in the sunlight. He had a clear face and a clean, neat nose. These features, along with the light blue eyes, worked together to show surprise at Pete's words.

"You're the only person I've told, Pearl. Except Dusty, over at the Saddleback. He's good as gold. I told him damn little anyway, and I ran into Flagg and Gregory right after that. But Flagg seems to know something."

"He didn't get anything from me."

"Do you think he knew this fellow Burr?"

"Chances are. Burr got around, and he probably would have tapped on Flagg's gate."

"Does he have a gate?"

"No, that's just an expression. Actually, I don't know what he has, because I haven't been by his place. But he strikes me as the type that would live in a big house with an iron railing all around. Like in the cities. If a peddler wants in, he's got to tap on the iron gate."

"Oh. This fellow Gregory that was with him said he was the gatekeeper."

"Probably comes from the city, then, or been there. Maybe thinks he's clever."

Pete reflected for a quick moment. "He seems to think that." Then Pete's thought looped back to the main subject. "I just wonder if Flagg has something to do with Burr getting killed. He didn't say anything outright, but he dropped little hints that made me think he knew about the girl."

"Could be."

"How long has it been since you first heard about this stolen horse ring and the King?"

Pearl put out his lower lip. "Oh, a year or more."

"And Flagg came into the country some time after that?"

"As near as I know. Probably six months later."

"Then there's a good chance he knows this fellow Grant."

"Could be. I don't know anyone who says he knows Grant, but like I said before, anyone who knows him will keep his mouth shut."

"Well, I don't like the looks of it."

"I don't blame you. Neither do I." Pearl squared his shoulders and stretched back his elbows. He didn't wear a vest or carry a watch, so the sun fell broadly on his grey flannel shirt. He relaxed his arms, then smiled as he pushed his hat back farther. "You don't ever want to trust a horse dealer. Not all the way."

Pete laughed. He was sure he could trust Pearl. The old horse trader wouldn't have made the joke if he didn't think so himself.

Chapter Seven

Pete rode out of the Flat Rock while the afternoon was still warm. The saddled horse that was tied to the snubbing post gave the wide eye to Star and Chub as they passed by.

Along with the chunk of antelope haunch, Pete carried a piece of advice from Pearl: "Get that girl to a safe place, but don't lose track of her." That was a good idea. He had already been thinking along those lines, but hearing it from Pearl helped him decide. He would rest the horses at camp overnight, and come morning they would take the wide way around to Laramie.

He would want to keep track of her in case he needed a witness about the shooting. She could also identify the third man, which could be useful to Pete or to the law, depending on how things developed. He pictured Rosy and smiled. She was a fine girl, and he'd also like to keep track of her just to get to know her better.

He was happy to see her when he rode into camp, and she had a bright smile for him. She looked over the second horse but did not say anything as Pete dismounted.

"Brought you a horse to ride," he said. He ducked under Star's head, stood between the two horses, and brought Chub forward.

Rosy stepped towards the horse and laid her hand on his jaw, then patted the sleek neck. "Is he a boy?"

"He's a gelding. Just about all these ranch horses are."

Rosy nodded. She was looking at the horse's eye, and her lips were moving as if she was speaking silently to the animal. Pete had the impression it was Spanish, but whatever it was, it wasn't more than a few syllables.

Pete spoke again. "I borrowed him from a friend at the ranch. Real gentle horse. Should be easy to ride."

"I like him," she said.

Pete handed her the lead rope. "I also got you some duds." He ducked back under Star's head and went to the hind end of the saddle, where he untied his jacket and the small bundle of clothing. He was going to hand her the clothing to put away, and then he realized it might seem like he was treating her like a servant. So he handed her Star's reins and said, "Let me set these over on the bedroll."

When Pete got back to her, Rosy was holding Star's reins with her right hand while she held Chub's lead rope with her left and scratched his throat beneath the jaws.

"You like horses?" he asked, taking the reins back.

"Oh, yes."

"That's good. I think tomorrow we'll take a ride."

She looked at him. "Where?"

He motioned with his head. "Back to Laramie, I think. You remember I told you about a man with a beard?"

"Yes."

"Well, I ran into him again today, and I think he's got an idea that you're out here with me. At any rate, he seems interested in everything I'm up to."

"So you want to go back to town." She transferred the lead rope to her right hand and patted Chub's forehead with her left.

"I want to take you there, where it should be safer. Safer for you, and probably for me, too. Then I'll take this horse back to my friend Dusty, and I might poke around to see if I can get a better idea of what I'm up against."

Their eyes met, and she nodded. "Do you want me to stay there?"

"I'd sure like it if you could just lay low for a while."

"In a hotel?"

Pete hesitated. "I know a . . . a girl . . . that I think we can trust."

"That's fine. That's better than being in a hotel room by myself."

"I hope so." Pete scraped his lower teeth against his upper lip. "I don't know what to think about this fellow with the beard," he said. He looked at her, and at her nod he continued. "His name's Flagg. I think I told you that. Well, today he had another man along with him. His name is Logan Gregory. Does that sound familiar at all?"

She shook her head.

"He works for Flagg. And I have a hunch they might both be workin' for the King."

Her head raised half an inch.

"You remember I told you about Pearl. He's the old horse trader. Good man. Well, he says the King is someone named Grant who never comes out in the open. For all I know, this fellow Flagg could be the King, but he came here after this stolen horse trouble was already started. And he goes around and meets people like he was runnin' for office." Pete screwed up his mouth and then relaxed it. "But he raises horses, so it's logical he knew Burr and knows the King, whoever in the hell he is."

Rosy shrugged. Pete could tell from her expression that she was following his line but didn't have any suggestions.

Pete went on. "Now this other fellow he had

with him, this Logan Gregory, I think he could be the third man."

"The one with the horses?"

"Uh-huh."

Her face showed a pained expression.

"You said the third one had a clean face?" He waved his hand in front of his own mouth.

"Yes. He didn't have a mustache or a beard."

"This jasper doesn't, either. Let's see what else." Pete summoned up a picture of Gregory in a yellow shirt and black vest. "How was he dressed? What color shirt did he have on?"

She drew her eyebrows together and then relaxed them. "I think it was a grey, like yours, or maybe a clear blue."

"No vest?"

"I don't remember. He had a jacket."

Pete thought again. Then he remembered the leather thong. Looking at the white cord around Rosy's neck, he said, "This fella had a leather string around his neck." He motioned with his free left hand. "Leather. Like a cord."

She shook her head. "I don't know. He had a handkerchief." She spread her open hand downward below her chin.

"What color?"

"Red."

"Well, that's somethin' to look for." Pete gazed at her throat, and even though he was working on the puzzle, he noticed the blue dress and the white cord against her pretty brown skin. He shook his head. "Anything else about him? What color were his eyes?"

"Brown. And brown hair."

"Anything else?"

"He was different from the other two."

Pete thought, *Yes, he kept his pants on*. Then he said, "In what way?"

"He was clean. He was shaved, and he was cleaner than they were." She looked directly at Pete. "He was more like you."

"Well, thanks. I guess that's a compliment. Those other two, they were a little older and a little dirtier." He looked down at the loose ends of the reins and bit his lip. "I don't know what else," he said. "I suppose we should go ahead and put these horses out to graze. Then we can fix up something to eat. Pearl gave me some antelope meat."

They had a good meal of biscuits and broiled antelope, followed by coffee and the remaining can of peaches. As they ate, Pete noticed Rosy's features. He liked her long dark eyelashes, her straight nose, her neat lips. The dark skin was smooth and clean from her forehead down to her neckline. It all went together—the dark hair, the clear features, the even-toned skin. She was pretty.

After the dinner, Pete rolled a cigarette and lit it. Rosy offered to go for water, and he nodded. He sat on his rock as she walked away from camp, her hips moving gracefully beneath the dress.

John D. Nesbitt

Pete shook his head. He had to keep his mind straight. Someone had good reason to want to find that girl. It might be Flagg and Gregory. Whoever it was, they probably knew that keeping track of Pete could lead them to the girl. If he hid the girl in town, they would be less likely to find her. And they might get tired of keeping a lookout for him, if that's what they were doing.

He took another pull on the cigarette and glanced at the rock she had been sitting on. He didn't even like to let her this far out of sight, but she needed her privacy from time to time. This seemed like a safe place. No one had been around, not that he could see, and he had also kept a good eye on his backtrail today, with plenty of switchbacks and dodges.

He thought of Rosy. He could imagine her kneeling at the water, filling the canteen. When he had been down the mountain on his ride earlier in the day, he had thought of her back here at camp. With some people, it seemed like the only time they existed was when they were around. A fellow didn't bother to think of them the rest of the time. Oh, sure, if he got right down to it, he knew that their lives were going on. That chicken-necked clerk at the Edwards Hotel, for example—he was probably carrying on his daily routine. And the crib girl Ruby, wherever she had skeedaddled to—she was probably somewhere, and still up to the things she did the best. But with Rosy it was more complete. All he had to do was think about her, and he got a full sense of her alive and warm and breathing in another place. And smiling. Maybe splashing water on her face, sweetening herself up before she came back to camp.

Pete listened. It was too quiet. He stood up, took a last drag on the cigarette, and tossed the butt into the coals of the campfire. As he settled his hat with his left hand, his right floated down to check the pistol.

He walked out of camp and down the hill. The country was steep enough here that a person couldn't see very far ahead as he went downhill. About halfway to the stream he saw her as she came into sight, carrying the dripping canteen. She saw him and smiled. She was a pretty sight as she walked up the hill in her blue dress. He let her stop to catch her breath when she got to the spot where he waited. The rise and fall of her chest created a graceful motion in the still afternoon. They stood there for a couple of minutes, looking at the country around and below them. Then he carried the canteen as they walked back to camp together.

"Did you see anything?"

"No."

"I almost got worried."

Their hands brushed together once as they walked up the hill. Pete wanted to put his arm around her, but again he reined in the impulse.

When they were back at camp he brought out the bundle of clothes and then found the clean undershirt among his other things. He handed the items to her as he sat down on his rock next to hers. "These ought to be more comfortable for riding than what you've got on. They might not fit so good, but they should be all right."

She sorted through the clothing in her lap. Then she looked at him and smiled. "Thank you," she said.

That night they slept warm and comfortable again, in the same arrangement as the night before. Pete kissed her once on the back of her right cheek and put his hand on her waist. From there it was a soft easy fall into sleep.

In the morning they were up and moving at dawn. Rosy went off to change clothes while Pete fanned up a fire with his hat. She came back and stood in front of him with her arms straight out like a scarecrow. The shirt was loose, with the sleeves in thick folds above her wrists. The pants were baggy also, with cuffs covering all but the tips of her shoes.

Her eyes were shining, and when she and Pete looked at each other, they both laughed.

"Will it work?" he asked.

"I think so."

He nodded as she lowered her arms. There was a cozy air about it all. He liked the idea of her wearing his clothes. Then a detail occurred to him. "Where's the dress?"

"I left it by the saddle."

It did not take long to have breakfast and to

break camp. They were on the trail before the sun had risen very high. It was a cool, dry morning, and their breaths were visible on the air. If there had been dew, there would have been a frost. Rosy wore the wool gloves. Pete's hands were warm from saddling the horses, so he rode bare-handed as the morning sun spread the new day's light upon the horses and riders.

They took the long way around, veering to the south, even beyond Pearl's ranch. Once they were down on the plains they would hook around to the northeast to head for Laramie.

The weather stayed fair and the horses didn't lag, so they were riding past the stone walls of the Territorial Penitentiary in Laramie by mid-afternoon. Pete kept them to the side streets, and after a little navigating he brought them to the side of a two-story frame building.

He helped Rosy down from the horse, as he had done on earlier stops during the day. "This is the place," he said.

Rosy looked up at the building. "I thought you were taking me to a lady's house."

"Well, I am. Sort of. This is a girl I know. I think we can trust her. I didn't know where else to go. If you wait here, I'll run up and see if she's in."

Rosy looked up at the building again and then back at Pete. Her face had taken on a hard look. "All right," she said.

Pete found Angel's room without any trouble. He had never been up on this floor in the afternoon, and it looked dull and dusty. He tapped on the door, and it opened a crack.

He tried to keep his voice low. "Angel. It's me, Pete. Can I come in?"

"I—I'm not ready yet. I'm just getting up. I need to freshen up, and—"

"I didn't come here for kootchie-koo," he said, even lower. "I need to ask you a favor."

"Well, come on in," she said. She opened the door and stepped aside, and as he walked in she said, "There's no one else here."

Angel was in a pink robe or housecoat that reached to her ankles. Her blonde hair was loose and falling down, and her pale face, which had been wiped clean of makeup, looked tired and puffy. Pete expected her to yawn, but she just looked at him.

"I'm sorry to bother you like this, Angel."

"No, that's fine," she said. Now her hand moved to cover her mouth as her chin stretched down. "What do you need?"

"It's a twisted-up story," he said, "but the long and the short of it is that I've got a girl who's in trouble and she needs a place to hole up for a while."

Angel's eyebrows went up and then down. "How old is this girl?"

"Oh, don't worry about that. She's about your age."

"When's her baby due?"

"What?"

"You said she was in trouble."

"No, not that. Well, she is in trouble, but not that way. She's a witness to a murder."

Angel's eyes widened. "And someone's looking for her? Why don't you take her to the sheriff?"

"I don't think any of this has gone to the law yet."

Angel looked straight at him. "What kind of girl is she?"

"She's a good girl. You'll love her. Her name's Rosy." As he said it, he realized he pronounced it with a *z*, as in "lazy."

"Where's she from?"

"From down New Mexico way."

"Oh. Is she dark?"

"Well, yes. Does that matter?"

"No, not at all. We just don't have any of them here."

Pete paused to try to get the words right. "I just want a place for her to stay, that's all. She's a good girl. And I thought I could trust you." He looked at Angel. "I knew I could."

"Sure you can, Pete. You know that." She paused a moment. "We can find a place for her. Give me a few minutes to get my things together, and then bring her up."

Pete took Angel's hand. There was no electricity in the air, and she didn't seem to expect a kiss, so he just shook her hand. "Thanks, Angel. I knew I could count on you."

When he got back down to the street, Pete couldn't find Rosy. The two horses were tied as he had left them, but she was nowhere in sight. As he stood with his hands on his hips he heard footsteps behind him, and he turned to see Rosy walking out of the same door he had just come through.

She was wearing the blue dress again. "I found a bathroom," she said, smiling. She handed him the clothes she had been wearing. "Thank you."

"Sure," he said. He took a quick look at her in this new setting. The dress was not tight or revealing. She looked like a good girl, all right. He hated to leave her here in Laramie, but he knew she would be safer in town than out on the mountain—for the time being, at least. He took the clothes and tied them onto the back of Chub's saddle. He would re-pack them later. "We can go on up in a few minutes."

She was standing in the sunlight, and in spite of having been on the trail for three days she looked firm and fresh. He had the urge to hug and kiss her, but he held back and said, "Everything should be fine here. I'll be back in a couple of days. How's that sound?"

"That's fine." As she looked at him, her eyes began to shine with moisture. "Thank you," she said. "You've been very good to me. Not every man would do that."

He took a deep breath and kept his own eyes from watering. He held out his hand, and she met him with hers. "You helped me be that way," he said. "I hope I get to see more of you before long."

"I hope so, too."

When they got to the second floor and knocked on Angel's door, she opened it wide. "Come on in," she said. "I'm going to the washroom. I'll be right back." She was still wearing the housecoat and had a bundle in her left arm.

Not wanting to delay introductions, Pete spoke up. "This is Rosy. Rosy, this is Angel."

Angel's blue eyes went soft as she looked at Rosy and took her hand. "Hello, Rosy." She pronounced the name as Pete did.

Rosy smiled and said, "Pleased to meet you."

Angel left the two of them standing in the room, and she closed the door on the way out.

As Pete looked at Rosy he felt his smile vanish.

Her face looked harder than it had when she had first seen the hotel. She spoke in a low voice. "Why did you bring me here?"

"It's the safest place I knew of. And I don't know all that many people to begin with."

She nodded towards the bed. "I know what kind of place this is, and I don't do any of this."

"No, no, no. No one expects you to. I told Angel you were a good girl. She knows you wouldn't ever set foot in here on your own. But I think the two of you will get to understand each other just fine."

"I think we understand each other already. It was in our eyes when we met."

"What do you mean? It looked to me like she liked you."

"Yes, but I know about these places, Pete. I didn't ever go to the room, but I know about them." Her face was not as hard as it was before, but it was serious.

He felt his mouth getting dry. "What-all do you know?"

Her eyebrows went up and down. "I thought you knew already. I thought you could tell."

He shook his head. "Tell what?"

"I used to dance. In Las Cruces."

"You mean you were a dance-hall girl?"

She nodded. "But I never went to the room."

"You just danced? Two bits a dance, fifty dances a night? That sort of thing?" A ready image came to Pete's mind.

"Sometimes it was only ten cents, but yes. It was hard work, with drunk men, sometimes very dirty ones."

Pete nodded. He imagined it was hard work, putting up with men like Flint, and worse. As he looked at Rosy, a feeling washed through him. With this new knowledge he had, she seemed more real than ever. She seemed to grow in his eyes, to take on more personality, more dimension, than before. He felt his eyes going moist now.

"Do you still respect me?" she asked.

He took her in his arms and kissed her forehead. He looked across the top of her beautiful black hair and said, "Of course I do. A woman's a woman."

"I danced," she said. "Sometimes my legs were so tired I thought I would have to quit. But I kept working."

"And you thought I knew, or had guessed?"

"I didn't think so before. But when we came into the room, I thought maybe you guessed, and that was why you brought me here."

"No, not at all." Then a thought went through his mind. "Was it true what you told me about your father?"

"Yes. But I also wanted to leave New Mexico because of this other thing." She took a couple of slow breaths, and her body moved in his arms. "If you've worked like I have, you think everyone can see it on you, even though you know they can't."

"So how was it that Elwood Burr met you?"

"We went through an agency. Maybe he knew, but he didn't meet me in a dance hall. But he probably thought something, and that's why he brought me here like he did."

"But you never went to the room?" He held her back and looked her in the eyes.

She looked straight back at him. "Never. And I won't start now."

He bent his head to kiss her, and as he closed his eyes he had a swirling image of the lovely dark lashes, the silky black hair, the white cord against the smooth bronze skin. He brought his lips to meet hers, and she gave him back his kiss, warm and moist and brief as they stood in Angel's room.

Chapter Eight

A woman is a woman. Pete ran the phrase through his mind as he rode out of Laramie, over the plank bridge that crossed the Laramie River and on past the penitentiary. *A woman is a woman.* Even if she had something in her past, she was still the person he had come to know and like. He wanted to prove his respect for her. That was why he had been willing to let her move his hand to her waist. And now it was why he would continue to treat her gently and not try for the kootchie-koo. They had taken a big jump in knowing each other and knowing what each other knew: that she had danced and he had been to the room with Angel. Rosy said she had never gone to the room. It occurred to Pete that she did not say she had never been with a man. But that didn't matter. What mattered was what they recognized in one another. If he was going to show his trust and respect, it meant he couldn't treat her in a way that suggested he thought she was like Angel.

He felt a pang as he thought about Angel. He would be locked out of that, now, too—for as long as he was interested in Rosy. All three of them would naturally see it that way, given the circumstances. Well, that was all right. A man shouldn't think he could have it both ways. Still, there was nothing wrong with Angel. She was all right, and even more so if she was helping take care of Rosy.

With Rosy, he couldn't act with the same assumptions he had with Angel. But that didn't mean he thought Rosy was better. Just different. Even if she had gone to the room, he would still be feeling what he felt now. Maybe even more. If a woman said no, that was it until she said otherwise. That was how he felt, even if a woman used it on him so she could work him, and that didn't seem to be the case with Rosy. The main thing was, he had to show her he believed in her.

She wasn't better than Angel. Just in a different situation. *A woman is a woman.* He had thought that line about Angel before he had said it to Rosy. He believed it in both cases. He still did. He knew he didn't really believe it about all women, but he did about both of these. He had

116

to. If a man didn't believe in a woman, there was nothing between them.

As far as that went, he had heard of good women coming out of those places. As the stories had it, many a man had found a woman he liked in a place like that and had taken her away and made a wife out of her. That worked with women who could leave that life and that had the wife in them. It was a pretty idea, to pick a woman up out of the street and make a better life for her. It made a fellow feel good to think about it. Pete had even thought, distantly, about Angel in those ways. Then again, he had heard a story or two about a married man who went sporting around and found his wife in one of those places, much to the surprise of both of them. Pete figured those stories for jokes, but he also knew that jokes came from somewhere.

Pete looked at the sky. If he made good time, he could reach the Saddleback by nightfall. There was no place he had to be, and the supplies he had bought in Laramie would last him that much longer if he turned in at the ranch. He felt a smile play at the corners of his mouth. The nights weren't getting any warmer, and if he had to sleep by himself, he might as well go for a night in his old bunk.

The men were just getting up from the table when Pete arrived at the bunkhouse. Dusty offered to help Pete put away the horses, and Chicago Thorne assured him there was plenty of slumgullion in the pot. Pete thanked him and went outside with Dusty.

They put Chub in the pasture and Star in the corral. There were two wagon horses already in the corral. Dusty explained that he and Elk Legs were leaving in the morning. They would take the light spring wagon and leave it in town, and Chicago would pick it up in a few days when he went in for supplies.

"Seems like he'd ride in with you."

Dusty's blue eyes danced. "You know Thorne. Likes to do things on his own."

"I suppose." Dusk was gathering as Pete glanced at the bunkhouse. "Heard anything?"

"No, not really. How about yourself?"

"Not much. I met up with Flagg again right after I left here. He seems to get around. He had his hired man with him. Name of Logan Gregory."

Dusty shook his head. "Haven't heard of him."

"Neither has Pearl. But he says he knows Flagg. That's about it."

Dusty took the toothpick from his mouth. "I take it you got your errand done."

Pete smiled. "Yep. I think I have her in a safe place for the time being."

"That's good. I hope this all gets cleared up without any big trouble."

Pete laughed.

"What's that?"

"I just thought of Clell, that old badger that

118

works for Pearl. He says it's all up to the 'beggaries' of fate."

Dusty grinned. "I guess it is."

Back in the bunkhouse, Pete sat at the table as Dusty went to his bunk.

Chicago Thorne set down a dish of stew. "There's more," he said as he turned and went back to the kitchen.

"Thanks."

Thorne came back with a tin plate of biscuits. He was wearing an apron, and since, like the rest of the men, he had his hat off for the evening, he looked less like a pistol cartridge than usual. "Still camped on the mountain?"

Pete looked up and met Thorne's gaze. "Not at the moment. Thought I might stay here tonight, if that's all right."

"Sure is."

"I thought so. I already put my horse in the corral."

"Sure is," Thorne repeated. Then he said, "All done with the other horse?"

Pete reached for a biscuit. "Oh, yeah. I just needed him for a day, to scoot some stuff around."

"Uh-huh." Thorne turned and walked back to the kitchen.

Pete ate his dish of stew without talking. Dusty and Elk Legs were at their bunks, going through their gear. Pete imagined they would leave some things here over the winter and were giving their bags a last once-over. He heard the sound of tableware rattling in the dishpan. Pete could see Thorne with his back turned to the table. The dirty white apron strap was tied across the back of the black vest. Thorne was all right, he thought. He might play his cards pretty close to the green, but he made sure everyone got taken care of.

Thorne looked over his shoulder from washing dishes. "Care for some more?"

"In a minute."

Thorne shook his hands over the dishpan, then walked toward the table, wiping his hands on the apron. He arched the two halves of his continuous eyebrow, and Pete nodded. Thorne was back in a moment with a second dish of stew. As he set it down he asked, "When do your greenhorns come in?"

"In a little over a week." He looked up at Chicago, then glanced at the food and said, "Thanks."

Pete ate the second serving more slowly. Thorne came back out from the kitchen and sat down at the table. He still had on the apron, so Pete assumed he was waiting for the last dish.

"Met that fellow Flagg again," Pete said without looking up.

"Oh."

"Had his hired man with him. Logan Gregory." Pete looked at Thorne.

Thorne's eyes widened a little. "Didn't know he had one."

"Then I went to Pearl's. I asked him some more about these stolen horses."

"And what does Pearl say?" Thorne pushed his chair away from the table, dug underneath the apron and pulled out his watch. He opened it and closed it and then started winding it.

Pete finished chewing and swallowed. "He says there's talk about someone named Grant. Supposed to be the boss of it all."

"Might be."

"Have you heard any of this?"

"That's all I've done, is heard."

"Do you know what he looks like?."

"I've heard he's short and pudgy and grey-headed, but I couldn't say." Thorne put the watch away.

"Well, I sure wonder who's who in all of this." Pete leaned over the bowl and took a bite of biscuit.

"Hard to say." After a pause, Thorne added, "You seem pretty interested in these stolen horses. Is there something we ought to know about?"

"Not really. But if it's goin' on, it's not good for any of us. And I'm plannin' to go out with some pilgrims and a string of rented horses, so I'd like to know what I should be lookin' out for."

Thorne brushed his apron and smoothed it down. "Makes sense." Then he stood up as Pete set the spoon down in the empty dish. "More?"

"No more, Chicago. But thanks. That was good grub."

"And welcome to it." Thorne picked up the dish and the empty tin plate and returned to the kitchen.

Shortly after sunrise the next morning, Dusty and Elk Legs were all set for town. The men shook hands all around, wished each other good luck for the winter, and parted ways. Pete, who had already re-packed his gear and saddled Star, headed for the foothills as if he were returning to the mountain.

He turned in the saddle when he reached the first rise above the Saddleback headquarters. Thorne had gone back inside or into the barn, and the wagon had already dipped out of sight to the east.

Pete settled back in the saddle and gave rein to Star. He decided to loop on out west and then back to the east, skirting the trail that led straight south but ending up at Pearl's Flat Rock Ranch again. He wanted to return a favor for the grub Pearl had given him, and he wanted to ask about Thorne's description of Grant.

The day was coming on now, and it looked like the weather might be changing. There was a high cloud cover, and the day was likely to be cool and hazy. It was good weather for traveling, but it might not be for long.

When Pete reached the Flat Rock headquarters, he could hear voices and a rasping noise from the creek down below. He rode towards the noise, past the new corral. A young horse, a solid chestnut about four years old, was standing inside with nothing on it—no saddle or halter. The colt trotted halfway around the corral and stopped even with Star and Pete, then stuck its chin over the top railing and whinnied.

Star gave out a short snuffle as Pete nudged him towards the human sounds. The horse went through the brush and brought Pete out thirty yards from Flint and Clell, who were at the two ends of a buck saw and working their way through a dead cottonwood. The saw wheezed and rasped as the two men worked it back and forth. When they saw Pete they waved, then went back to their motion.

Pete stopped about fifteen yards away and curled his right leg up over his saddle horn. He rolled a cigarette as he watched the two men slicing the saw through the log. Then it broke through, and a round fell off the end of the log to join half a dozen other rounds on the ground.

Clell hooked the saw onto a stub on the log, and the two men sauntered over to Pete, who stuck the cigarette in his mouth and got down from the horse.

"Layin' in some firewood?" he asked as he shook hands with Flint, then stood back.

"Yeah. This is the hardest damn cottonwood I ever cut through."

"I tell him it should burn good," said Clell.

"Howdy, Pete." He reached out his spotted hand.

Pete stepped forward to shake it, then stepped back. "I suppose you'll tell me Pearl's not around," he said with a grin, "and try to get me to take a turn."

"Have at it." Flint threw back his head as he dug the makings out of his shirt pocket. He troughed a paper and shook tobacco grains into it.

Clell smiled with his flat lips and tipped his hat back on his forehead. "You're too quick for us, Pete. We'll git you next time." The old man dragged his left cuff across his forehead, then took the little cloth bag that Flint handed him. He peeled out a paper and loosened the neck of the bag. "Just passin' through?"

"Sort of. Thought I'd swing by here and drop off something I found for you."

Clell looked up from shaking out the tobacco. "What's that?"

"I found you a bottle in my travels."

"Empty or full?" The old man raised the pouch, hooked the yellow drawstring with his tongue, gummed down on it, and pulled the bag shut.

"Full, of course. I've been to town."

"Them's the best kind. We got a bundance of empty ones. But a full one. That's a good boy." Clell tossed the bag to Flint and began to roll the cigarette. "Didn't you see Pearl?"

"No."

Flint spoke up as he whooshed out a cloud of smoke. "He's probably in the shithouse."

Pete could see Flint but still looked at Clell. "I came down here where I heard voices."

Clell licked across the edge of the paper. "He's up around the cabin somewhere."

Pete nodded. There was nothing to be in a hurry about. He watched as Clell stuck the cigarette in the side of his toothless mouth and lit it.

Flint piped up. "Guess what Pearl found."

Clell's mouth looked like a carp's as he blew out the smoke. He held the cigarette between two fingers as he said, "Didn't your ma ever give you a titty to suck on?"

Flint scowled and looked at his cigarette. "I suppose so. Why?"

Pete imagined Clell meant that the kid was trying to get attention. The answer was a little different, although it might have included what Pete thought.

"It was to keep your mouth shut. If Pearl wants to tell him, he'll tell him." Clell laid the end of the cigarette back on his lower lip and took another drag. Then he turned to Pete and, with the cigarette bobbing, said, "Kid likes to hear himself talk. Got the brains of a shithouse mouse."

Pete almost laughed. Clell's comment seemed double-barbed without his knowing it. But the remark about Flint's mother had seemed to hurt, and it made Pete not want to laugh. Flint

125

was still looking at his feet, so Pete spoke to him. "That was some good-tasting antelope you shot, Flint."

"Thanks." Flint looked up. He drew on his cigarette and as he exhaled he said, "And thanks for bringin' the full one."

"Glad to." Pete turned to Clell. "I suppose I should go find Pearl. Leave you gents to your work."

"You bet. And thanks, Pete."

"Any time." Pete dropped his cigarette butt and ground it with his heel. Then he turned and led Star up out of the creek bottom and towards the cabin. He heard a pinging sound from the stable, which was off to the left of the cabin. He headed in that direction and met Pearl, who was stepping out into the sunlight with an ax in his hands.

After they had exchanged greetings and a handshake, Pearl held the ax with its head up. "Put in some wedges so the boys can swing away."

Pete pushed out his lips and nodded. Then he presented Pearl with the full bottle, and the two of them walked towards the cabin. As Pete was tying Star to the hitch rail he said, "I may have picked up something about this mystery fellow Grant."

Pearl, with the whiskey bottle in one hand and the neck of the ax in the other, straightened up and said, "Oh, really?"

"Uh-huh. I got it from Chicago Thorne. He

says he hasn't seen Grant but he heard he was a short, pudgy man with grey hair."

Pearl wrinkled his nose. "That doesn't go along with anything I've heard, but it doesn't contradict anything, either." He looked at Pete. "But it might be true."

Pete shrugged.

"Let me put this bottle inside," Pearl said, "and I'll tell you what I found." Pearl set the ax by the doorway on his way in, and he was back out in a moment. He bent and picked up a stick that lay by the front door. "Let's sit down over here," he said, indicating a bench along the front of the cabin, which faced east.

When they were seated, Pearl looked around, then looked at Pete. "I think I found a way station."

"A what?"

"A place for these horse thieves to pen up horses. A holding pen."

"Is that right? Where is it?"

"Probably not very far from where you had it out with those two jaybirds." Pearl bent over and with the stick he traced a map in the dirt. "Here's Mineral Creek. Here's where the old Frenchman had his cabin. All right. Go up on this bluff on the east side of the creek, and look straight down. You can't see it from anywhere else because of all the growth. But you can see it from here, plain as day. Once you know where it is, you can go back down and find a little trail leading into it and out of it through the quakies. Probably from when they built it."

"Uh-huh. Is there a cabin there?"

"No, just a pen. It looks like a place where they can leave horses for a little while and then move 'em on."

"Sounds like a good thing to know about."

Pearl looked at him and nodded. "You bet it is. If any horses are missing, we can go there first. We can keep an eye on it at other times, too, and we might be able to pinhole someone who's in on it."

"Has there been a lot of horses through there?"

"Didn't look like it. My thinking is they've got these holding pens all along the way from Montana to Colorado, about a day's ride from one to the next. That way they can move 'em along and stay out of sight when they need to."

Pete looked at the map and nodded slowly.

Pearl waved with the stick. "I think most of the horses go south, from Montana and here on down to Colorado and who knows where after that. After a little rest here, it's less than a day's push to get a small herd of horses to Colorado."

"They're not driving off big herds, then?"

"I don't know, but from the little I've seen and heard, it doesn't seem like it. And right now, with all these horses being turned out after roundup, they can pick the best."

"And no one's likely to notice much until spring."

"That's it."

"You're not missin' any head?"

"Not yet. I figure they'll hit me later, just before they move out of this area."

"Why is that?"

"Someone like me who's got just horses is likely to keep a closer eye on 'em. You take some outfit like yours, the Saddleback, and no one's likely to worry about anything but the horses they keep right at headquarters. They feed them through the winter, and the rest of 'em fend for themselves. Isn't that right?"

"It makes sense," Pete said. "I don't think you could steal horses from under Chicago Thorne's nose, but if you get out a ways, why, nobody's there to say boo."

"Exactly. I think there'll be horses movin' through here for the next few months, and if we keep our eyes open, we might catch a fish."

"And if we catch the right one, then that girl and I won't have to worry any more."

"That's right."

Pete found the spot with no trouble. When he reached the bluff he dismounted and walked his horse along the edge. Every few steps he leaned out to look more directly below, but all he saw was quaking aspens. Then suddenly he was right over it, and it was easy to see, just like Pearl said. It was laid out in front of him, fifty feet below. He crouched at the edge of the bluff to study it.

It was a four-sided pole corral, diamond-shaped, with the narrower angles pointed east and west. It had that shape because it was built where there had been a clearing in the aspens. All the poles looked to be pine, which would be easy to find as deadfall in the nearby dark timber. Pairs of upright posts had been set in the ground, and then the rails had been laid inside, ends overlapping on top of one another. The sides looked like they were each about thirty feet long. There was no gate, so the rails in one section would have to be taken down or slid aside to let horses in or out. The pen looked like it could hold at least fifteen head.

Pete looked across the mountain as it rose to the west. The bluff would be visible from over there, but once a person got up the mountain high enough to see over the aspens, he wouldn't have the angle to see down into the pen. It seemed like a pretty clever piece of work. He looked down into it again and did not see any droppings or evidence that the pen had been used.

"What's it look like?" The sharp voice in back of him sent a jolt of fear through him, and he nearly lurched, which might have been dangerous at the edge of the bluff. But he steeled himself. He knew that voice. The man might have a gun leveled on him, so he would have to get up slow and easy, with his hands away from his body. Star was to his left, so he rose slowly and turned to his right. It was the voice he thought it was. There was Logan Gregory, fifteen feet away.

"It looks like a holding pen." Pete looked at the other man. He wasn't holding a gun or even wearing one, so the immediate fear went away. Pete remembered to observe how Gregory was dressed. He was wearing a tan shirt and a sheepskin vest. Pete looked at his neck. There was no handkerchief, and the leather thong was visible.

"A holding pen?"

"Uh-huh. Like someone might use to hold a few head of stock." Pete thought the other man might not know much about livestock. Then he thought, for a man who spent most of his time at the ranch, this one got out and around the country quite a bit. "Come take a look at it. Or did you already see it?"

"I've seen it, but I'll look some more." He walked over and stood next to Pete. "What do you say it's for?"

"Someone might hold a few head of cattle in it. Or horses. Especially horses, if they were movin' 'em somewhere."

"Something like a little jail, isn't it? No gate."

"It'll hold horses."

Gregory stretched his back and straightened himself to his full height, which was two inches taller than Pete. Then he said, "Stone walls do not a prison make."

"How's that?"

"I said, 'Stone walls do not a prison make.'"

"Meanin' stone walls don't mean it's a prison, or a prison doesn't have to have stone walls?"

"Either way, now that you put it like that." Gregory was looking down at the pen. "But my main meaning was, I don't see how you can know it's for horses if there aren't any in it." When Gregory spoke faster as he did now, the Texas accent came through more clearly.

"I don't." Pete looked sideways. The taller man was strong-looking, as before, and he conveyed a sense of physical power. He wore leather gloves again today, and the sheepskin vest gave his back a rounded, muscular look. His features were hard and square but not gross or fleshy.

Gregory shrugged and looked at Pete. "Who are we to say what it's for, eh?"

Pete turned down the corners of his mouth. "It damn sure ain't a bathtub."

"No, it's not that." Gregory pushed his hat back on his head.

Something in the gesture reminded Pete of a phrase. *You don't ever want to trust a horse dealer. Not all the way.* Thinking to catch his man off guard, he said, "Have you seen Pearl?"

Gregory answered right away. "I don't know Pearl."

Pete believed him, and he felt a twinge of guilt for his moment of suspicion. He knew he could trust Pearl. It had just been a false connection for a moment. He asked, "Then how do you happen to be here?"

"I was looking for you."

"When did you see this pen before?"

"When I walked up. Stand back where I was. You can see it from there." Gregory settled his hat back into its usual position.

Pete nodded. "That's all right." He didn't want to seem anxious to walk away from the edge, so he fished into his pocket and brought out his tobacco. With a gesture he offered the bag to Gregory.

The other man shook his head, short and brief.

Pete opened the bag and looked up at Gregory. "Why were you looking for me?"

"There's someone who'd like to talk to you."

"Your boss? Mr. Flagg?"

"No. His wife."

Chapter Nine

It was a good two-hour ride to the Black Diamond Ranch. Although Logan Gregory seemed to enjoy delivering theatrical lines and maneuvering for position in the conversation, he didn't turn out to be a sociable talker. Very little chit-chat passed between the two men, so Pete had plenty of long moments to think.

If Gregory had been looking for him, he had done a good job of finding him in the big wide open. He might have followed Pete to the Flat Rock and then to the spot where he had come up from behind. He didn't say he hadn't seen Pearl; he said he didn't know him.

Pete thought back to the day he had shot the two men. If Gregory was the third man, he was holding good cards and was in good table position. He would have Pete counted down to the dirtiest little deuce. Except for Rosy and where she was. That was Pete's hole card.

If it was Flagg's wife who wanted to see Pete, it would be interesting to find out why, as well as why Flagg was out of the picture—if he was. It was quite possible that Gregory, in his secret sense of humor, might tell him a woman wanted to see him, and then deliver him to the bearded master. Who could tell? Gregory always seemed to be smirking at Pete, but the general tone didn't seem sinister. Not yet.

They came to the Black Diamond Ranch just about where Pete thought it should be. It was on the plain, in rolling country that seemed flat for miles but that held dips and surprises. Many times in the plains country, Pete had ridden right onto range cattle or antelope. As the boys said, it was mighty poor country for rustling. Or as Clell had said once, you could ride the country all day long and not see anyone, but stop and get down to make a deposit, and that's when you could expect someone to ride up.

The headquarters lay down in a swale between two grassy dunes. The riders came at the little group of buildings from the north. There was no broad entrance or iron railing, just a brown ribbon of dusty road that wound into the yard. The ranch house was a simple, square, clapboard building that was showing the weather. It had the type of roof that was common in this country—no gables, but rather a pyramid made of four triangles sloping up from the side walls. The roof was covered in wood shingles, with tin strips on the ridges and a round tin ball for a cap. Off to the west was a straggly row of low elms, half dead in the upper branches. To the east was a long, low barn that presumably housed the Black Diamond stables. Pete could see one corner of a corral on the off side, which faced south. In back of the house, also to the south, stood a couple of outbuildings, one of which was large enough to be a bunkhouse.

They tied their horses to a hitching rail in front of the house. That seemed like a good sign to Pete. The horses were in plain view, and the visit was likely to be a brief one. Pete looked up at the sky. It was still hazy, but he could see the sun overhead at a little past the midday position. Then Gregory, taking off his hat, opened the door and conducted Pete inside.

Pete stood for a moment in the vestibule, a small room in itself for hats and coats and boots with a double door against winter drafts. As he took off his hat he closed his eyes to adjust to the darkness, then opened them and walked through the door into the sitting room.

A dark-haired woman in a dark dress rose from the sofa.

Gregory motioned towards her with a sweep of his right arm. "Mrs. Flagg." Then with a backward wave of his left he said, "Mr. Garnett."

The woman stepped forward and gave Pete

her hand. As he took it, their eyes met. Something rippled, an undertone of familiarity, although he did not recognize the woman. He took in quite a bit in his first look. She had dark, wavy hair that hung almost to her shoulders. Her face had the fair complexion of a woman who did not labor in the sun. The green eyes were comforting, the plucked eyebrows cordial, the red lips and white teeth friendly as she said, "Thank you for coming."

His gaze lingered on her face. "It's my pleasure."

"Please sit down," she said. Then she turned and moved back towards the sofa.

Pete felt her woman-ness there in the sitting room. She was a handsome woman, perhaps her husband's age or a little younger. She had a trim figure—a full, high bosom, a flat stomach or at least not pooching out, and shapely hips. The dress was loose but not billowy. She and Pete sat down at the same time, and as they did, he noticed her ankles. They were nice-looking, not thick like he had seen on farm wives, and not skinny like he had seen on some older women of the night. Whenever he looked over a woman before going to the room, he noticed the ankles.

They faced each other again, at a distance of ten feet in a room that was lighter than the vestibule but darker than the day outside. Pete could see a few grey hairs, all singles. She must have caught his look, for she raised her left hand to smooth her hair. Pete's eyes followed the hand as it went back to her lap and joined the other. They were smooth, young-looking hands.

"I hope you find me an easy person to talk to," she began.

Pete nodded.

"I hope you don't think I'm too forward. I think of it as being frank and direct. And time has a wingéd chariot."

Pete nodded again.

"I understand you know my husband."

"We've met a couple of times."

"And I understand you might be in trouble."

"I don't know."

"I suppose you have some idea." She looked at Gregory, who had been standing out of the way. "I do say, Logan. Here we are, having brought Mr. Garnett all this way and then not offering him a refreshment." She turned her amiable eyes towards Pete and asked, "Do you drink brandy?"

"Yes, I do."

She looked up and smiled at Gregory, who dipped his head forward and back in a miniature version of a bow, then left the room through a door to her left.

She looked back at Pete, and her eyes sparkled. "He understands me so well." She tilted her head. "Where were we? Oh, yes. Before I go any further, let me tell you that I don't know the details of my husband's affairs—his business—

but Logan has told me you might be in trouble."

"He might know more than I do."

"Well, I want to warn you—if that is still necessary." She looked at her hands, then back at him. "And I want to help you. If you can help me."

Pete took a deep breath. "Go ahead."

"You say you've met my husband. Did you ever meet him before?"

"I can't *say* that I did." Pete felt himself wince.

"Do you think you did?"

Pete glanced at the doorway that Gregory had gone through to leave the room.

"Don't worry. Logan is the one who told me. My husband has very good reasons for not saying a word of it to me."

"Where is he, by the way?"

"My husband? He said he had to go to Denver." She paused for a second. "I think that's where you might have met him."

Pete's mouth was dry and he could feel himself shaking.

This was what she meant when she said he might be in trouble, and he thought she was right. There was no sense in holding out, though. He cleared his throat. "In the Edwards Hotel."

She smiled, and it soothed him.

He went on. "I didn't actually meet him."

"But he was in the room."

"There was a man who was there and went out the window. When I met your husband I

139

thought it might be the same person."

"That's how you can help me."

Pete raised his eyebrows.

"It was my room."

Pete licked his lips. "I went in there by mistake."

She smiled and nodded. "Oh, I know. That's all been explained." She separated her hands and laid her left hand open in her lap. "Let me tell you a little more." She put her hands back together and looked directly at Pete. "I was trying to leave my husband, and he was trying to stop me. His strategy got interrupted."

Pete nodded as he breathed in and out through his nose.

"I'm going to have to be frank with you, even if it doesn't cast a very favorable light on me."

"Go ahead."

She took a deep breath, looked down at her hands, back up at Pete, and spoke slowly. "There was another man. Call him my lover. We met a few times. We exchanged letters." She paused. "My husband found some letters. Not all of them, but enough to send him into a rage—a terrible, terrible fit. He burned the letters, he burned my dresses, he burned my books. The other man had given me some books. My husband didn't know which ones, so he burned everything he suspected. Then he"—she looked at the doorway—"he imposed himself on me."

Pete shook his head slowly.

She looked at her hands, which were still together. "After that, I felt that I had to leave. I went to Denver. The other man was supposed to meet me, but he didn't." She looked up. "I received a letter at the hotel. He was bowing out. Meanwhile my husband followed me, and after that you know as much as I do."

"Where did you live then?"

"In Grand Junction."

"Your husband never has let on that he was there?"

She shook her head. "Not in the slightest. And if I were to suggest it, it would only bring up the whole subject of my infidelity, which he can turn into a nightmare. So we both act as if he wasn't there that day."

Pete thought. "Who was the other man, the one in the room?"

"Mace. My husband's right-hand man. His trusted servant."

"How could he pretend he wasn't there, if this fellow Mace was?"

"Mace was in love with me, or at least carried a flame. He knew about the letters, and it must have excited him to know I would consider another man."

Probably like to get one in on the boss, too. Then Pete said aloud, "So it ended up looking like his work. The breaking-in."

"Yes, and it was made out to be my fault. It was poor Mace, all gone wrong because of me, the evil temptress."

141

"Did you—"

"I never gave him any encouragement. He came slinking around with his hints and insinuations, and I could tell he was fascinated, nearly obsessed, but I turned him away every time."

"Why would he help your husband?"

"It kept him close to the center of the affair. I think he wanted a hand in it, one way or the other."

Pete gave a low whistle.

She nodded. "They took it and twisted it into something sick."

"Yet you went back to him."

"Yes," she said. "And I'm not proud of it." She took a deliberate breath. "He bent me to his will." She looked at Pete with her left eyebrow arched. "A man has many ways to keep a woman in bondage. He has used more than one."

"Did you go back to Grand Junction?"

"No. He was all repentance for what he had done before I left—though he never mentioned details—and he said we could go someplace else and make a new start. But I wouldn't say that trust has been a major asset between us. We went to Thermopolis, and that's where we were until we came here."

It seemed to Pete as if the conversation had come full circle. "What would you like me to do?" he asked.

She looked at him with a softened face. "I

would like you to be willing to say he was the other man in the room."

Pete swallowed. "Wouldn't that make things worse for me?"

"I can guarantee you it won't."

Pete could feel himself being drawn in. It was like quicksand. No, it was softer than that, like a feather bed. It was as if someone had wrapped a blanket around his shoulders. He looked at her. He did not think she was bad. And she was a woman. That was what pulled at him, her woman-ness and the soft sympathy it called up in him. He could have gone to the sofa on impulse, or to his knees in front of the sofa. That was how it pulled on him. Still he sat in the chair, rotating his hat brim with his two hands.

Her guarantee was gallant, but there was no real assurance that it would hold up. He could just get himself in worse. And furthermore, there was Gregory. He was somewhere on the other side of the open doorway. He could be working confidences both ways between the boss and the Mrs. Pete looked up from his hat and found the woman looking at him, waiting.

"I don't think I can do it, Mrs. Flagg. In the first place, I didn't see the man well enough to say positively that it was your husband. We'd have to have it from him, and I doubt we'd get it."

"I think you're right on that last point."

"In the second place, I think I'd just get tangled in deeper."

"I have to respect you for that," she said, and her green eyes were moist as she blinked. She breathed in through her nose, and her chest rose gently. "I do wish Logan would bring us a drink." She turned her head towards the doorway and raised her voice. "Oh, Logan."

In less than a minute he appeared with a tray, which held a glass decanter and three small glasses. As he set it on the low table at the far end of the sofa, to the woman's right, Pete saw the leather thong. It was lying on the tray, and it had a skeleton key attached by a slip noose.

Gregory poured brandy into the three glasses, then offered the tray to the lady and to Pete. He set the tray back on the table, pulled a chair near, and sat down beneath a set of antlers. Pete noticed that Gregory had taken off his gloves, and there was a scar on the back of his left hand.

With right thumb and forefinger, Gregory raised his glass and said, "To our health." As the other two raised their glasses, he finished the toast by saying, "All of us."

Pete sipped on his brandy. He saw Gregory pick up the leather cord and drape the empty loop end over his right index finger, push the loop towards the palm with the middle finger, and drop the key through the loop. He tightened the noose on his finger and let the key dangle down from his palm. Then he waved his hand and gave it a flick, and the key sailed around the back of his hand and landed in his palm. His

144

lips pressed together and his eyebrows flicked a quarter of an inch. He exchanged a glance with the lady and took another sip of his drink. Then he stood up.

"I ought to water the horses," he said, looking at Pete. "They've cooled down enough. I suppose yours could use a drink."

Pete looked up at him. It all seemed very businesslike. "That would be fine."

Gregory walked out through the vestibule, leaving Pete and the woman by themselves in the room.

After a moment of silence she said, "I trust that you still see me in the capacity of a friend."

Pete looked at her. Again there seemed to be something familiar about the woman. "Yes."

"You give me a strange look."

Pete felt a tingling in the air. "I feel as if I know you from somewhere."

She nodded, and the green eyes went softer than before. "You should. We *have* met."

Pete felt a bold current go through him. He felt a lightness in the head. It was as if he were sinking again. "When?"

"That same day."

Pete looked at her. His head still seemed to be swimming, but the knowledge came to him. "In the room."

"Yes. The other room."

He shook his head. "I wouldn't expect to find you there." He remembered her now, a firm woman but a little older, who gave him a whirl before he went to the Edwards Hotel. He had forgotten that the two events were on the same day so close together. The enormity of shooting the intruder had pushed the preliminary event far back in his mind, but he remembered it now. She had done him good in that little visit. He looked at her and asked, "What were you doing there?"

"I needed money," she said. "And the man I was supposed to meet had left me stranded." She looked serious, almost timid, as she sipped on her brandy. "I wasn't going to say anything unless I thought you recognized me. I'm afraid this makes me look even worse than before."

"No," he said. *A woman's a woman,* he thought. Then he added, aloud, "You had a reason for doing it."

"More than one," she said.

He felt his pulse jump as he looked closely.

"Not pleasure, though. Well, it was pleasant enough with you, I remember that. But my main reason was business."

Pete hesitated. "And beyond that?"

"Beyond that, I suppose it was to spite him, to get even for what he had done. And also, I simply wanted to get away from him."

"And that was your ticket."

"I thought so, and I thought it would put a personal distance between us as well."

"Does your husband know?"

"He knows I had a few turns, but he doesn't know with whom. I think it made him even more driven to take me back. Regain his mastery, you know."

Pete motioned with his head towards the yard. "How about . . . ?"

"Logan? Oh, no. I wouldn't breathe a word of it to him. It would drive him crazy, too."

Pete sensed an answer to a question he had had at the back of his mind. Gregory must have some intimate knowledge of the lady also. Pete remembered standing next to him at the edge of the bluff, and now he had a clearer sense of why the man could be dangerous. "You feel you can trust him, though?"

"Oh, yes," she said. "He's devoted to me. He'll serve the master until the time is ready."

That must be part of the guarantee, Pete thought. She wanted him to help tie her husband's hands, and then she would skip with Gregory. They wanted Pete to give them something solid for blackmailing the master. He was glad he had declined. He looked at her, and the eyes were shining. She wasn't working it like she could, but the pull was still there. And although he wasn't going over, he liked the feeling of their shared knowledge. "When did you know I was the same man?" he asked.

Her eyes twinkled. "When you walked into the room with your hat off."

"Back then, did you have any idea?"

"From the description, I thought a good hand could have done both."

They both laughed. It was a good, hearty, nervous laugh.

Pete shook his head. Then he nodded. "I'm not sure if this would have changed my answer to your question."

"I was afraid it might complicate things. And like I said, I thought I would wait to see if you recognized me."

"That was good of you. It kept everything clean. I appreciate it." He paused. "And I think I will stick by my original answer."

"I would think so." She looked down at the glass she held in her lap. Then she looked up and said, "And I do hope we can be friends."

"I don't know why not," he said. "That's how we started."

They laughed again, shorter this time.

Then they both lapsed into silence until a question occurred to Pete. "Mrs. Flagg," he began.

"Please call me Lenore."

"Well, all right, if you'll call me Pete." He paused and then went on. "Lenore, have you and your husband ever had any children?"

The eyebrows arched over the pretty eyes. "No."

Pete nodded once. That helped explain the firm midsection. And the pert bosom, too—no baby had fed there. Pete found himself looking in that direction.

"Not at all," she went on. "It's not that I couldn't, but that I haven't wanted to." She shook her head. "This is bitter of me, Pete, but I wouldn't give that man a child, and I wouldn't give the world a child of his." She looked at him, as if to be sure of him. "You know, it's in a woman to want to have a baby, but as long as that man is in my life, I have to deny myself having a baby with anyone." She let out a long breath. "I'll tell you more. You probably wonder why I ever married him."

"Well, yes. I imagine he was a different man then."

"I should say so. But even then he was the serpent in the garden. I just didn't know it."

"Uh-huh."

She shifted on the sofa. "I was young," she said. "I had a sweetheart. Then"—she paused—"my present husband came along. He was all smiles and charm. I didn't see the seething maniac beneath the surface. I couldn't." She opened her right hand, palm up, in Pete's direction. "You probably know him as a polite man, smooth-mannered. But there's at least two of him. In public he can be very charming, but in private it's as if a little door opens and the other one comes out. He has a poisoned soul." She waved her hand. "But enough of that. Back to my story. I met him, and he was kind and considerate. Then my sweetheart went away—to California—and my new admirer tricked me. He fabricated a telegram saying that my dear boy was dead, and then when I was all down and broken-hearted, he talked me into marrying him."

"And then you found out it wasn't true."

"Of course I did. But by then it was too late. I did what I could." She paused and sipped on her brandy, and with something of a gloating air, she said, "I closed off his manly privileges." Then she sank ever so slightly. "Then by and by he took them anyway."

"You mean he—"

"He imposed himself on me."

Pete felt the anger rising in him. His mind flashed the scene of the two men who had tried that with Rosy. "I don't know why men have to do it that way," he said, "when it can be so much nicer."

"It's not meant to be nice when they do it that way. It's meant to be dirty. Degrading." She looked at him squarely. "It's not for pleasure, not the kind you would imagine. It's for control. To keep the woman down and make her feel dirty."

Pete sat silent. He felt like a wide-eyed, openmouthed boy.

"The woman knows it," she said. "She can tell from the way he acts, from the look in his eye."

Pete recalled the look on the fish-belly-man's face. She was right. It was the look of a man intent on overpowering a woman, not the happy look a man should have if he was about to go through the golden gate. He nodded. "I know. I've seen it."

"That's too bad."

"I killed him." Pete was looking at the floor. He could feel the grimace on his face, and he realized he may have said too much.

"Oh." After a pause she added, "It's too bad you didn't get the other one before he went out the window."

Pete pulled himself together. She must not know the details about the two men in the clearing. She thought he meant the look on the face of the man he had shot in the room. There was no need to say any more, so he just said, "Uh-huh."

"The master," she said. "But his day will come." She breathed deeply again and said, "So, no, Pete, there haven't been any children. And there won't be." Then she gave a genuine smirk. "Especially the way things are right now. I have his 'manly privileges' closed off again."

That should keep his pot a-boilin'. Then Pete said aloud, "Don't you worry? Like before?"

She smiled. "Not right now. I told him if he touches me I'll squeal like a rabbit in a trap." She motioned with her head. "With Logan around, he doesn't want to look bad. He knows Logan would come running."

"What if he fires him?"

"Frankly, I think he's a little afraid of Logan, though he wouldn't admit it. And besides, he's been having a hard time keeping men. They just up and leave."

Pete decided to ask a surprise question. "Lenore," he said.

"Yes?"

"What do you know about the King?"

She shrugged. "There isn't one right now. Just the Queen. Victoria. The only king I know of is on the chessboard. The master has a fine set of pieces in onyx. *His* set. He can go through everything of mine, but I've never touched his chess set."

Pete said nothing.

"There I go," she said. "You must think I'm a bitter old woman."

"Not so old," he answered back, smiling. "And you have reason to be bitter."

"I thank you for seeing it that way."

"It's the least I could do. And we *are* friends."

She smiled. "Yes, we are. And I hope we stay that way."

Pete sensed that she was bringing the interview to a close. "I'm glad you sent for me. It's been an interesting visit."

"Yes, it has, and thank you for coming." She rose and held out her hand.

He stood up and moved forward to meet her. There was a charge in the air and a warm, firm pressure in her hand. He felt he could have weakened even at this moment, but he knew they both wanted it to be this way—clean and free.

Her face was kind as she looked at him and said, "Don't be afraid to see me again."

"I won't," he said.

As he stepped out into the daylight and put his hat on his head, he saw Gregory come out of the barn with Star. Pete supposed the man had put his own horse away and could now finish his drink.

Pete took the reins from Gregory, then glanced at the house and back at the hired man. "When does your boss come back?" he asked.

"In a couple of days." Then Gregory put on the look that suggested he was enjoying his private joke. He wrinkled his left nostril and pointed his right thumb at his own chest, just below the place where the leather thong disappeared beneath the shirt. "Make no mistake about me," he said. "I'm my own master."

Pete mounted up and rode away. Beyond the clip-clop of Star's hooves he heard the door of the ranch house open and close.

Chapter Ten

With the Black Diamond Ranch behind him, Pete was on his own. The sport hunters would not arrive for another week yet, so he had no immediate obligations. He could stay where he wanted, come and go as he pleased. It disturbed him that Logan Gregory had found him so easily, so far from the ranch where Flagg had said he stayed most of the time. Then it occurred to him that he hadn't been all that careful himself. When he had had the girl to look out for, he had taken all of the precautions—found a remote camp, was careful with fires, switched his trail, and kept a weather eye out for anything unusual. With the girl gone, safely tucked away, he didn't feel any close danger. Still, he thought, he had killed two men just a few days earlier—

four days, as he thought back—and someone would be wanting him to pay the fiddler.

There was also the old business from the Edwards Hotel. It was something he had done by reflex, without thinking, but it was coming back to haunt him now like an ancient grudge. Flagg might want to get even; at the least, he knew he was under the risk of being identified as the intruder who got away.

For as much as Pete had tried to bury that incident in his memory, he had always known he had done it. For five years he had carried the knowledge that it might come back to him in some way, but since he felt he had been in the right—indeed, still felt that way—he had not consciously known any fear.

Now he thought of Lenore, the Mrs. There was something that struck deep there. Her revelation that they had met before had seemed so calm, and had been so layered over with the charm of their present meeting, that Pete had felt the knowledge only on a physical level. When he realized he had been with that desirable woman before, it was as if he became aware of it with his body. There had been a yearning to return, plus an awareness that he had to fight that urge.

No longer in her presence and therefore not feeling the immediate enchantment, he could see their first meeting more clearly as a completed act. It was something he had done, truly without thinking. With the magnitude of the encounter in Room 9 not long afterwards, it had been buried. Now it was dug up, like a buried gem. It hadn't deteriorated; it was still all in one piece.

That was it. He felt now what he hadn't been aware of when he was in her presence. The earlier meeting was something that couldn't be undone. In that way it was like the killings. Yet it was different, because it was something he didn't realize he had done, and now he did. Before today he had known he had been to bed with a woman. Now he knew who it was and what relation she had to him.

Pete felt a chill run through him. It was like a bad dream, the dreams he used to have before he ever killed a man. In those dreams, he would be aware of having killed someone and buried the body. But in the dream he could not remember the act itself, the killing. It was something already done and with no reason he could attach to it. Those dreams had come half a dozen times, years ago. He remembered one thing in particular. In the shadowed world of his dreams, the act he knew of but could not remember doing was always the same. The dreams changed in their setting and color, but they always seemed to refer back to the same original act.

Something already done without his knowing it—that was how it now seemed with Lenore, the Mrs. He could not remember the details of her body, or the sensation of what he some-

times called getting wet, or the afterglow that
came from the release with a woman. All he remembered was that he had gone to the room
with a well-kept older woman and that it had
been good. Now he knew what it added up to.

Uh-huh. And as he had sat there in the sitting
room with his hat in his hands, he had wanted
to go back. Return to the scene of the crime, as
they said. If he had done one good thing, it was
keeping his seat. Sure. And if she had wanted,
she could have pulled him anyway.

He was in it anyway, he thought. He was in
this thing deep. Even if Flagg didn't know he
had gotten wet with the Mrs., Pete did. Flagg
would probably not know enough to want to get
even on that score, and his wife did not seem
inclined to use the earlier meeting for any pur-
poses of her own, but Pete knew he was tied
deeply to both of those moments in the past.

It was like a bug. You could carry it with you
and not know you had it until the little fella
started to burn.

He was in it. He was like that young chestnut
he saw in Pearl's new corral. Run around in cir-
cles, nostrils flaring. Look through the planks,
up over the top. He'd been in there longer than
he could remember, but now he knew it. What
he didn't know was how to get out.

Pete rode into the mountains. Gregory was
not after him, not at the moment anyway, and
Flagg was supposed to be in Denver. Still, there

was the King and anyone who might be out on his orders. Pete was going to have to be careful. It was big country up here, and a man always had half of it at his back.

He looked at the sky. It was getting greyer. There would be snow before long, he could tell. If the snow stayed around, it would cover old tracks and preserve new ones. If it melted, it made the leaves quieter. It also made the ground soft, so whether it stayed or melted, it made tracking easier for whoever was doing the hunting. He thought about tracking after a snowmelt. He recalled images of deer and elk tracks that had been pressed into damp earth, had been snowed on, and then had been revealed when the snow melted. Easy to read.

His thoughts drifted back towards Gregory, and he wondered again if the man had followed him for very long. He wondered how handy the hired man would be in the big country. Gregory seemed to have some of the city in him, but he didn't bounce around in the saddle or get lost in open country. Now that he thought of it, Pete wondered why Gregory hadn't mentioned hunting or wished him luck again. For all Gregory knew, Pete was still putting together a hunting trip.

He thought of going past that place where the aspens met the pines, where he had been scouting to begin with. Then he decided not to. Whoever the third man was, he had probably gone back and taken care of the bodies. Someone had probably found Elwood Burr by now, too.

Pete decided to ride for the high country, up and over the top. He could let things settle, if only in his own mind. He was into the timbered country already. That was fine. He knew the open spots and the dark trails, and he could be over the top before nightfall.

A dry camp was the best camp if he wanted to drop out of sight. Common sense told him not to camp by water or build big fires. He thought of himself as being like a timber buck, picking a spot where he had a good lookout and not much at his back. Up and over the ridge and a little ways down, he found a spot that looked good. There was a rocky slope behind him, which would be noisy for anyone approaching. In front of him there was a screen of cedars. In the daytime he could picket his horse in the aspen trees below. It was similar to the camp he had shared with Rosy, except that it didn't have a rock overhang and it looked west instead of east. The other one had been a good camp, but he didn't want to use it up. If he camped there now, he might put it on the map for someone else.

After dropping his gear and picketing the horse, he gathered rocks and put them in a circle to build a fire pit. Then he gathered some dead sage and small cedar branches and built a fire. It was going to snow. He was glad he had the extra clothes, but he knew better than to dress too warm too soon. He laid out the saddle blanket, then the bedroll, the slicker on top of that, and the extra clothes under the covers. It would be warm enough like that.

Later that evening, after he had checked the horse and spread out the coals he had let burn down, he crawled into his nest. He lay on his side with his knees tucked up. It was not as cold up here as it would be when the cloud cover lifted. When it did, that would be when he would really miss Rosy. He thought of her on the other side of the mountain. She was probably in a warm room. Angel would take good care of her.

When he camped like this, he usually had the feeling of emptying out. On roundup he didn't, because there were men and work all around. But out here, life was reduced to a few things—tending to the horse, staying warm, managing the water and food. Everything else fell away.

Tonight, though, some of it stayed with him. He was on top of the world with openness all around him, but he knew he was still in the pen. Like that young horse, jolting around in a circle and stopping to stick his chin over the rail. He knew he had felt free, but when was the last time he had really been free?

Ten years, since he left home in Kansas? No, since then. Five years, before that day at the Edwards Hotel? No, before that. Uh-huh. Before Florence. Florence and the cub.

Pete let out a long, slow breath under the covers. Might as well. Go ahead and think about

it, let it out. For all the good it had done him
not to think about it.

Florence. Brown curly hair and white breasts,
nipples like pink pyramids, the smooth slope of
her stomach and the soft brown valley below.
Florence, his first love—Florence, who left him
feeling like the cub he was.

Seven years ago, almost eight. Pretty Florence, still a girl. Just a couple of years older
than Pete, married to a man over forty.

Tears splashing on the pillow. "He doesn't understand me. He's so much older. All he wants
is a chamber maid."

Pretty Florence, pyramids poked up in the
curtained daylight, blue eyes looking up at him.
Moist eyes. "You understand me. That's why it
seems so right." Soft and lovely Florence, her
body meeting his. "I love you. I love you." Her
breath in his ear. Her hands on his back.

His face next to hers, his nose on the pillow.
"I love you, Florence." His nose between the
pyramids as he kissed the hollow of her breast-
bone. "I love you, Florence."

Kissing the stomach above the soft valley.
"Oh, Pete. Oh, Pete."

The door breaking open—not breaking, really, but the key loud in the lock, and the loud
wrench of the knob, and the angry rush of the
door swinging open on the hand of Jacob Slater.

Huddled under the covers, side by side, Slater

standing at the foot of the bed like their father.

Naked with only a blanket to cover him.

"Get your clothes on. You're going home." Florence like a dog about to be beaten, Florence scooting out from under the covers, keeping her back to the angry man as she reached for her clothes.

Slater coming to Pete's side of the bed, looming over. No gunbelt. Just the large, open hands like winter gloves.

Naked with only a blanket to cover him, his proud manhood shriveled to a little worm.

The large hands coming down like sledgehammers on his temples. Nowhere to go. Clutch the blanket.

"You-dir-ty-lit-tle-cub." One syllable per slap, a spray from the man's mouth as he spit out the words. "You fil-thy-lit-tle-bas-tard."

Florence into her dress now, sobbing, not looking at Pete. Head lowered, looking up at her husband, her master.

"Let's go."

Naked under the blanket. Florence turning her back and leaving, the man following. The door still open with the key still in the lock.

Pretty Florence.

And the cub, in his shame. Thought he understood her, gave her a level of feeling she couldn't find with the old man. Just got him a slapping down. Could have gotten him killed.

* * *

Pete shook his head as he lay in the bedroll with his knees tucked up. Whenever the memory had come up he had tried to stifle it, the shame had been so strong. He had thought he was being considerate, and in the moment of his shame and hers too, she had walked out on him. Maybe there was no other way for her. It didn't matter. He was left alone in an empty room with an open door. When he thought he was putting that much into it, it came to nothing. It had been better not to think about it.

The boys said none of it was free. He guessed not. After that it had been easier not to get drawn in. Pay your way like a man, get wet and get out. Or so it seemed. It had gotten him in the pen anyway, as he saw it now. Gotten him back in and kept him there.

How long had he been in the pen? Since Florence. Since he was a cub. He had been nailing on planks since then and not known it. And this thing with Florence. It was just as well to get it out now and face up to it. Try to know it for what it was, and then see how to get out.

He lifted his head out from under the covers to breathe the chilly mountain air. It was going to snow. That was good.

It snowed that night, about four inches of early, wet snow. Pete knew it was easy to kill blue grouse on snow, so he got up early and went to the timber while it was still cold. Using a stick was a quiet way to get meat. He found a good stout piece of cedar an inch thick and a yard long, and after about an hour he found a bird nestled under a fir tree. Giving the stick a hard backhand fling, he got himself some fresh meat for breakfast. That was his way—make meat while it was easy, and save the supplies.

The snow melted in the afternoon as the sky cleared off and the sun came out. The sky was blue again, but the air was cool. Snow lingered in the shady spots, and by late afternoon the temperature began to fall again.

Pete did little during that day. He loafed and rested, enjoying the fire and the coffee. He wandered through the timber to scout for deer and elk. There were deer tracks, and he saw a few does and fawns. If there were big bucks around, they were holed up. More likely they were still higher up in the mountains just west, where the elk probably were.

He looked at the mountains to the west. A man could climb and climb and feel like he was on top of the world, and still it always seemed like there was a higher mountain yet. That was all right. A man didn't have to stand on them all. Just one at a time, and the one he was on at the moment was the good one. Maybe that was the difference between him and the mountain men. Some of those fur hunters weren't happy until they'd been on top of all the big ones. Pete shook his head. Climbing all those mountains and killing all those beaver wasn't in him. He guessed he was a cowhand at heart.

He stayed a second night at the dry camp, and

then he thought it would be good to move. It wouldn't do to stay in one place too long, if only because it gave him the jitters. The only thing was, he didn't have any place to go to next.

The weather wasn't getting any warmer as the morning progressed, so he decided to peel down and put on an undershirt. He would get a chill doing it, but he would be warmer afterwards. As he was pulling the shirt over his head, he was reminded of who wore it last. It carried a trace of Rosy.

That was a good idea. He could wander down and around and go check on her. If everything was fine there, maybe he could drift back and see what Pearl knew.

It was midday when he broke camp. He could take the long way around, pitch camp north and west of the Saddleback before dark, and ride into town early in the morning. He rubbed his hand across his cheek. That's right. Shave in the morning.

He found a good spot for a camp, a place he had seen before. There was an old fire pit in front of a rock face, with aspens all around. It hadn't snowed as much down here as up above, so the aspen leaves were still loud. And plenty had fallen in the past few days.

As he settled into his bedroll he thought tomorrow would be a good day. He could see Rosy, and Angel too. He might have a drink or two. How long had it been since he had had a drink? Oh, yes. With the Mrs. Glass of brandy. He tried to remember if he had seen Gregory actually take a drink. Yes, he had.

Pete remembered having a drink with Pearl one time. It was in town.

"Never trust a man who won't take a drink," Pearl said. He tossed off a shot of whiskey, then pushed back his hat and said, "And don't trust no one who does, either."

An image of Gregory's smirking face presented itself. *Don't worry*, thought Pete as he drifted into sleep. *I don't trust him either way.*

The King

Better to cast it in the belly of a whore than to fling it on the ground.

The one with the red hair. No. She turns her head this way, she looks like a strumpet. And the teeth.

Yes, the blonde one. Flouncy. And all that lace. Pretty, pretty. A cushion for the ride.

Sip slow. Make it last, this part too. Be sure to choose the best one. Look them over. Can't have them all, not this time. Choose one and take it all the way. Can't come back and say I want another. Maybe some other time. Long way from the kitchen to the bedroom.

Don't have any dark ones here. Little blonde is the prettiest. Cut that rump with a whip. Shouldn't touch her tongue to her lips like that.

Or maybe she should. Raises the Adam in me.
    Yes, yes. Look my way again, and that's it. Yes.
My little pearblossom. Yes, yes. Drive it in like a
dagger.

Chapter Eleven

Pete awoke with the feeling that he owed Elk Legs an apology. The long-legged cowpuncher used to take an occasional drink, but since Verna's death he hadn't touched liquor. Pete imagined that Elk Legs' abstaining was part of a process he was going through, as a way of honoring Verna's memory. Maybe Elk Legs would have a drink again some time after the monument was in place, but in the meanwhile Pete excused the mournful young man whenever Pearl's saying came to mind. Like a lot of Pearl's comments, the warning about a man who wouldn't drink was a joke with a serious undertone. A man who refused to drink might be afraid of what would come out after a drink or two; or he might be waiting to get an advantage on those who were bending the elbow. Neither of those possibilities seemed to apply to Elk Legs, and it didn't seem right to include him in a joke, so Pete usually made an exception for him when he thought about the saying. He had forgotten to do that last night, so he woke up feeling apologetic. By the time Pete had the morning fire blazing, he felt he had made things right with Elk Legs.

Thinking back, Pete remembered that he had recalled the saying while he was pondering Logan Gregory. Now as he thought it through again, he wondered what the key was for. From the way it had appeared on the tray, it seemed as if it went to a closet that held the liquor. It could well be that Flagg was not supposed to drink. Maybe liquor opened the door that the Mrs. had talked about. Or it could be the other way. Pete smiled. If Flagg entrusted the key to Logan to keep his wife from the brandy, it sure wasn't working. Pete turned down the corners of his mouth. If it was a key to a liquor closet, it was probably to restrict Flagg and not the Mrs.

Then again, there was a possibility that it was just a theatrical device, that its only relation to Gregory's line about being the gatekeeper was to keep Pete wondering. He shrugged. Regardless of the intention, that was the effect. It kept him wondering.

It was a chilly morning but a pretty one, with the first sounds of daybreak carried on the cold air. A couple of times he heard the quick flutter of bird wings, and from time to time he heard the patter of small animals—mice or squirrels, probably—in the dry leaves. From where he sat he could see Star on his picket, and he could hear the scuff of hooves as the horse shifted in his grazing. Pete enjoyed the warmth of the campfire and the smell of the coffee. He drank from one can while he heated water for shaving in the other.

He looked at the sky. Sunlight was not yet slanting down into his camp, but the sky above was brightening and he knew the day was moving forward. He was probably not going to get as early a start as he had hoped for, but if he took a wide trail around by the north, he would have a good chance of staying clear of people he didn't want to meet.

When he had finished his coffee and shaved, Pete went to fetch the horse. As always, he watched the ground ahead as well as the area around him. He stopped on reflex, then reflected on the image that had told him to stop. It was a rabbit, a dark-eyed cottontail, crouched beneath a juniper bush. Pete liked cottontails. He liked to watch them, and when he was out like this he often took one for a meal. When he stopped, then, it was to admire the rabbit and, simultaneously, to think how he would kill it if he needed to. His next response was the decision itself. Not now, he thought. He was on his way to town and wouldn't need camp meat for a little while.

The rabbit was about ten feet away with its ears laid halfway back and its dark eyes watching the human. Pete looked at the soft flecking of its coat, then the reddish brown fur behind the ears. The rabbit was getting ready for winter. It looked warm, a compact little parcel of life. Pete moved to change his course and go around the rabbit, but the animal bolted away. Pete continued in the same direction he had been walking.

The air was still cool when he led Star out of camp and onto the trail. The saddle leather was cold as he mounted up and settled in. Star moved out at a brisk walk, showing he had some bounce in him. Pete felt good, too—he felt the strength in his arms and legs, the spread of power through his chest, the good tight feeling of his stomach muscles. That little rest had done him good.

Star made good time down through the foothills and out across the plains, bringing them into Laramie well before noon. Pete kept to the side streets again, arriving once more at the place where he had taken Rosy. As he climbed the stairs he ran the back of his hand across his cheek. He was glad he had cleaned up.

He had to knock a couple of times to bring Angel to the door. She opened the door just a crack, then seeing who it was, she opened it to about the width of her body. She looked tired, with an almost grey cast to her face.

"Are you all right, Angel?"

"Sure. I'm fine. I just had a rough night, that's all." She looked at the floor.

"I'm sorry to bother you."

"That's all right. I'd invite you in, but I just don't feel good." She looked back up at Pete with a pained smile.

Pete looked at her. She must have had one or more rough customers the night before. "I'm sorry, Angel. But I'll tell you, right now I'm looking for Rosy."

Angel's ashen face relaxed and she gave a half-smile. "She's in room twelve. There's nobody in it right now, so that's where we put her up."

"Is she all right?"

"Oh, sure. But I think she's ready to leave."

"Oh?"

"I think she feels she's been here long enough. But you talk to her. She's a nice girl, Pete."

"She sure is. Well, I guess I'll go check on her and leave you to get some rest. I hope you get to feeling better."

"Oh, I will."

"Thanks for helping me, Angel."

"Any time, Pete. Take care of her."

"I will."

Pete tapped on the door of number 12, and right away he heard a voice on the other side. He recognized the hard *s*.

"Who is it?"

"It's me. Pete."

She opened the door and moved aside in a quick motion, so Pete stepped inside. She closed the door and stood back.

Pete glanced over her. She looked good in the blue dress. It looked as if she had washed and pressed it. "How are you?" he asked.

"I'm fine. A little worried, but fine."

"What's got you worried?"

"I saw the other man."

Pete felt himself flinch. "The third one? The one with the horses?"

She nodded. "Yesterday."

"Where was he?"

"On the street. I saw him from the window. But I knew it was him."

Pete ran a quick search in his mind. Chicago Thorne was supposed to have come to town. "No mustache?" He wiggled his fingers in front of his mouth.

She shook her head.

"How about the leather string?" He pointed at his neck.

"I couldn't see."

Pete gritted his teeth. "What was he doing?"

"He walked up and down the street. I think he was looking up at the windows. That's what I felt."

"Damn. I sure wish I knew who it was." He looked her in the eyes. "Did he come up here with any of the girls?"

She shrugged. "I don't know. I didn't see any of that."

Well, that's good. Pete looked at the floor and then back up at Rosy. "What do you think?"

"I want to get out of here."

He raised his eyebrows. "I can't say as I blame you." He paused to turn the idea over and then said, "I think we'd better wait till dark."

She nodded.

"What would you think about going back to the mountain for a few days?"

"That's fine," she said. "I felt safer there than I do here."

"Uh-huh." Pete thought for another moment. "I'll tell you what I think. You know I've got a camp trip comin' up."

"Yes."

"Well, I can get some of the gear now—a tent, some bedding, and a couple more things to cook with—from the fellow who fits me out. Then I can get a horse for you to ride, and a packhorse, and I can bring 'em by here at nightfall. What do you think?"

"That's good," she said. "I can be ready. Angel gave me some things. She knows I want to leave, so she gave me some clothes for riding a horse and to stay warm."

"They fit all right?"

"Yes. I tried them on."

"Sounds like you're ready, then."

She smiled. "I am."

"You look good, Rosy."

174

"Thank you. You do, too."

They moved towards each other, and he put his hands on the sides of her shoulders. She turned her head to let him kiss her on the cheek as she did the same to him. Then they were apart.

"I'll see you in a few hours," he said, touching his hat and turning for the door.

Once on the street, he realized there was no need to hurry even though he felt things were urgent. For one thing, he had plenty of time, and for another, he didn't want to give the impression that he was up to anything out of the ordinary. He decided to move his horse out onto the main street, where he could leave it tied up a few doors down from the hotel. Then he could go about his business on foot, in his own good time.

It all seemed like a clever plan until he was tying the horse to the hitching rail. He heard footsteps come to a stop behind him on the board sidewalk, and then he heard a voice he dreaded.

"Well, if it isn't my young friend with the dark horse."

Pete turned to look up at Flagg, and as he did so he caught the overhead sun in his face and felt himself squint. He pulled his hat brim forward, turning the gesture into a greeting as he said, "How do you do, Mr. Flagg?" He stepped up onto the sidewalk and turned to one side to cut out the glare of the sun.

"Just fine." Flagg made no motion to shake hands. He was holding a pair of leather riding gloves in his right hand, and he drew them to a rest in the open palm of his left hand. "Just fine," he repeated. "I was down to Denver and just got into town last night. I was getting ready to go to the ranch."

Pete made a point of glancing to either side. "Where's your hired man?"

"Oh, I'm sure he's at the ranch." Flagg smiled. "Why?"

"Oh, no reason. Just makin' talk." Pete took a full look at Flagg, who was standing in good light. He was neatly dressed, as before, with the black vest buttoned and the watch chain shining. The white shirt was clean and the beard was neat. As Pete's eyes met Flagg's, he felt that the other man had been looking him over as well. Then the eye contact relaxed. Pete remembered a question he had about Flagg.

"Could I offer to buy you a drink?" he asked, raising his voice just a little from before.

"No, thanks," answered Flagg. "I just had one. Actually, if the truth be known, I had two. And I've got a ride ahead of me."

Pete nodded. Then he noticed something that held his gaze for a few seconds. The beard had grey or white roots in it!

Flagg's voice startled him. "What did Pearl tell you?"

Pete shook his head. "Huh?"

"What did Pearl tell you?"

"About what?"

"About the bit for that horse."

Pete frowned and then remembered. "Oh, he said the horse looked all right as it was." He took a breath. "As it turns out, I'm not going to use that horse anyway." Pete flicked his glance at the beard again, to make sure he had seen clearly.

"Pearl knows best," Flagg said, with his definite air. "I just breed 'em and raise 'em." He smiled and the slate-grey eyes softened. "Pearl knows all their secrets."

Pete couldn't help smiling. Flagg was being gracious even if the modesty was false. He could just as well have tossed off a comment like Chicago Thorne's and called Pearl a two-bit horse trader. "Pearl's a good man," Pete said.

"The best." Flagg pulled the gloves through his left hand and tapped them against his thigh. "Well, I'd best be going. It's good to see you again, Garnett, and remember to drop by the Black Diamond some day in your wanderings."

"I'll do that. It's good to see you again, too."

Flagg touched his hat, and Pete did likewise. Flagg stepped down into the street while Pete, with his back to him, walked into a café and sat down to order coffee.

A dyed beard, that's what it was. That accounted for the age difference. Up until now, Pete had had trouble matching things up. There had been no beard before, and the man who had gone out the window was older-looking five years ago than this man was at the moment. He probably dyed his hair, too. Pete hadn't thought to check that detail, but the beard had been enough. Flagg had been away from home for a few days and it had grown out on him. Yes, that explained the difference. Pete had figured Flagg for being short of forty, and now it seemed as if he could be forty-five or so, which would match up. Pete thought about the Mrs. He still wouldn't put her over forty. He smiled. He would know more from a closer examination, but he didn't think he would take it.

Pete sipped on his coffee. This fellow Flagg was quite a study. He could put a man at ease. Pete did not doubt what the Mrs. had told him about her husband being a madman and a liar, yet Pete had been able to stand there and look Flagg in the face and treat him like the gentleman he seemed to be. Then he remembered something else she had said. *There's at least two of him.* Well, that made sense. Pete had met the nice one, and even though he had sensed a dangerous underside to the man, it was natural to respond to the personality he was faced with. If he ever met the other one, that would be a different look-out.

At least one thing seemed as certain as before. Flagg wasn't the third man in the thicket. The beard may have been dyed, but it was real.

Pete dawdled away a couple of hours, first in

the café and then in saddle shops. Then, when he figured Flagg was well on his way home to dye his beard, he went to see about leasing the horses and the camp outfit.

That transaction went off well enough, without any unusual questions. Pete merely let on that he would pick up some things now and the rest later. As he had done the year before, Pete laid down some money and agreed to pay the rest after the excursion was done. He led the horses four blocks back to downtown, where he tied them next to Star.

He still had over an hour to kill. He thought about having a drink and then decided not to. Like Flagg, he had a ride ahead of him. He wondered if Flagg had really had a drink or if he had just said he had. Pete smiled. *If the truth be known.* That was the way dyed-in-the-wool liars talked. That was all right. Whether Flagg had had a drink or not, or was supposed to or not, Pete didn't trust him any more than he trusted Gregory.

Rosy was ready to go in a drab wool coat, a flannel shirt, and a shotgun riding skirt. She carried a small cloth bag with a drawstring. "My other things," she said.

Darkness was setting in when they stepped out into the side street where Pete had brought the horses. Pete tied the cloth bag onto the back of Rosy's saddle, helped her aboard, and then got Star and the packhorse into motion.

His plan was to make it past the foothills the first night, then go up and over the top the next day. That would mean some daytime travel, but they should be in the higher country before the day was very far along. He didn't know how many pairs of eyes were on the lookout for him, but up until now he hadn't cut anyone else's trail farther up.

There was a half-moon up by the time they reached the little stream that Pete had in mind for their camp. By moonlight he unpacked and unsaddled the horses, then put them out on pickets. He decided he and Rosy could risk a fire this first night out, so he got a blaze going. Then he set up the tent. It was a simple affair, a pyramid shape with a square base and a center pole. He whittled a pole and got the tent pegged out and propped up in short order. The white tent would be visible for quite a ways in the daytime, but if they got some snow up on top it would blend in pretty well.

As they sat by the fire eating bread and cheese from town, Rosy asked Pete what his plans were.

"Well, I'll tell you, I don't have a real detailed plan. If we can find out who this fellow the King is, then we'll know who we're up against. I'd like to talk to Pearl about it again here pretty soon. His place isn't that far from here, as far as that goes, but he's got a couple of men there that I'd just as soon not know about you and where you are. So, my first plan is to get a good hideout, and then after that, maybe I can slip down here and see if there's anything we can do to get the King off our back." Pete looked into the coals of the fire. "Then as a separate matter, this fella Flagg, the one with the beard, he probably has some personal score he'd like to settle. But about all I can do there is just try to stay out of his way until he makes a move." Pete picked up a stick and pushed some unburned ends of firewood into the coals. "Pearl thinks if we keep our eyes open we can get a line on this King. If we can, that could put you and me both in the clear." He tapped the far end of the stick on the rock. "And like I said before, I'm not real anxious to go to the law at least until we can put a name on that third fella with the horses. Otherwise, it just puts both of us out in the open." He looked at her. "I guess you'd just as soon go back home and be done with all of it."

She shrugged. "Maybe. But I barely left."

He paused. "Do you think you like it here?"

"I don't know. I haven't seen much."

"No, I guess not. All you've seen is killin', and hidin' out, and the—uh, the hotel."

She nodded.

"I suppose that's quite a bit different, quite a change for you. You know, it's not all like that."

She looked at the fire as she spoke. "There are good people and bad people everywhere. But it's still different. Over there in New Mexico, with my people, it all goes together. The houses, the food, the way we dress, the music. It's the

181

way we are." She looked at Pete. "I don't even have my own clothes any more. Or soap. That man threw them away. But I'm still a Mexican girl, no matter where I live. I am what I am."

Pete nodded as he looked at her. She made sense. They could dress her up in his clothes or Angel's clothes, but she was her own person and she carried her own world around with her. "I suppose," he said, "from what we talked about the other day, you're not all fired up to go back to Las Cruces." He looked at her and she gave no response. "And you don't know yet if you like it here."

He could see her nodding faintly in the firelight.

"Well," he said, "did Angel treat you all right?"

"Oh, yes," she said, without much apparent emotion. "They brought me food, and they let me take a bath. And Angel gave me these clothes."

"But—"

"But you can't think I was happy there." She looked at Pete, and her eyes shone in the firelight. "You know, Angel was generous with me. But I think she's a little bit jealous."

Pete felt some pressure in the comment. He shook his head. "No, I don't have anything special going with her." He wanted to say more, but he didn't know how to say it. Then he thought that by not saying anything he might be putting pressure back on Rosy to ask a question. Better to muck through it himself, he thought. "You see, Rosy," he began, "I know Angel and all of that, but as long as I'm gettin' to know you, I'm not goin' to have anything to do with her."

She looked at him, still without much expression.

"That's just the way it is—with me, anyway."

"How about her?"

"The only time there's been anything between us, I've gone to her. And I'm not goin' there. Not now. Maybe not ever again."

Rosy looked at the fire. "Too many men are the other way. They want more than one woman. They're afraid to promise themselves to just one. And then when they do, they have to have another one anyway."

"I know. They think it makes 'em free. But really"—he thought for a second—"it's a kind of jail." He poked at the coals. "And we've got enough things hemmin' us in without lookin' for more."

She gave a half-smile and nodded.

"I'll tell you," he said. "If we can get these other things straightened out . . ." He faltered.

"Yes?"

"Well, if we can get out of jail, we just might want to stay out."

"Have you ever been in jail?" she asked.

"No, but there's all kinds."

"I understood that. And I agree with you."

As he pushed the coals together, Pete's thoughts looped back to a small point Rosy had made about staying in the hotel. It occurred to

183

him that Rosy might like a kettle of warm water to clean up.

When he offered she seemed pleased, so he dipped some water from the stream and set the bail-handled kettle in the coals. Before long it was warm, and he lifted it from the fire pit. Then he went to check the horses, to give her a few moments to herself.

That night they slept double again, clothed as before, his right hand on her waist. He heard the horses moving around on their pickets. The weather was getting colder, that was for sure. One good thing was that it killed off the bugs. Made it easier on the horses. He was glad he thought of the warm water. She really seemed to appreciate it. She must have gotten some soap from Angel. She smelled clean and warm under the blankets, and the cold weather was clean, too, and Star wasn't stamping and shaking to keep the bugs off, just a clean-smelling woman in the tent and the shift of hooves on the grass that smelled like warm soap.

The King

I could have killed him. Maybe should have. Either time, same way. Front bead right between the shoulder blades. Raise my shoulder and the rear sight moves up his back and lines up with the bead. Nice and steady, not a squint and a jerk. Dump him right out of the saddle.

Have to wait now, though. No hurry. Easy to

kill any time. Like a barnyard calf. A mooncalf. Easy. When the time is right. When he has the girl with him.

Should have killed him back then. A quick job in a dark room. Just trying to keep my marriage together. Would have saved a lot of bother. Blundering little fool.

It'll come back around. Back into Papa's hands. For all he's done. I will be justified.

Chapter Twelve

Pete woke up. There had been a human noise outside the tent. There was an empty place where Rosy had been, but he had a sense that she hadn't been gone long. On the other nights they had camped she had gotten up in the early morning like this, so it seemed normal. This morning he had registered the knowledge at some level and continued to sleep comfortably. Until the noise—it was out of place, and it didn't fit well with her not being in the tent.

He rolled out of the warm bed into the cold morning, put on his hat and his boots, knelt to put on his coat, and ducked through the tent flap into the grey outside. The saddles and other tack were right where he had stacked them the night before, covered with a canvas manty. He reached under the canvas and pulled his saddle gun out of the scabbard. Then he stood and listened. There were no more human noises, but he heard what sounded like horses moving away at a fast walk.

A few quick steps took him to the spot where he had picketed the horses. All three were gone. Someone had waited in the first grey light of morning—probably had the horses untied and ready to go when they nabbed the girl. He looked around. There was no sense in calling out, and good reasons not to.

He shook his head to clear it. He needed to think through this. He still had a full sense of Rosy—warm and clean and close—but she was gone just like that. He was on foot. There was no point in trying to follow. They could cover ground much faster on horses, and they might even be waiting for him. He frowned. There was nothing to do if he stayed put, and it would just make him a sitting duck anyway. The best thing to do was hoof it to Pearl's.

He waited a few more minutes to see if Rosy would come back to camp, but his better sense told him not to hope for it. The day was getting lighter. No sense waiting any longer, he thought. He rolled the bedding back into two bedrolls and went on to strike the tent and fold it up. He snugged up the camp kit of grub and utensils, then tucked all the gear next to the saddles under the canvas. Pete looked around the campsite. It was hard to know what to expect.

If someone came back, it would be easy to steal the outfit, but at least now with it all packed up there was not an open invitation for them to wreck it. Pete shrugged, picked up the rifle, and started walking toward Pearl's ranch.

Pete figured it was about five miles across country. He decided to go on a direct march and take his chances at someone seeing him. Being on foot was poor business, and the sooner he got mounted, the better.

The sun was climbing in the east by the time he topped the last rise and looked down into the headquarters of the Flat Rock. Smoke was curling up out of the chimney, and he imagined the boys were having a last cup of coffee while they waited for the morning to warm up.

As Pete walked down into the ranch yard, the little black goat came out under a corral railing and looked at him.

The goat spoke and Pete answered, trying to imitate the "Meh-enh-enh-enh." As Pete got near the cabin, he called out. "Anyone home?"

The door opened and Flint appeared in socks and tousled hair, squinting into the sun. "Yo, Pete. Didn't hear you ride up. Where's your horse?"

"Good question."

Flint's face seemed to drop. He turned and said something toward the interior of the cabin. Then he turned back to face Pete, motioned for him to come on in, and disappeared inside.

Pete walked into the cabin and set his rifle

inside the doorway. The interior of the cabin smelled of tobacco smoke and cooked bacon. The three men were seated in their usual places at the table, in dim light with a haze of smoke. None of them was wearing a hat, and everything seemed relaxed as Pete sat down.

Pearl spoke first. "What's in the wind, Pete?"

"Someone raided my camp just before sunup. Made off with three horses."

Clell hit the table with his fist. "Sons of bitches. You see, Pearl?"

"Uh-huh," Pearl answered. Then he gave Pete what seemed like a knowing look and asked, "Did they get anything else?"

Pete looked straight back at him. "Yes, they did."

"By God," Clell cried out. "Damn me if I wouldn't like to shoot one of them fellers. Git me a horse thief before I die."

Flint finished licking his cigarette and spit out a tobacco grain. "You damn right," he said. "We knew this was gonna happen. I just been waitin'." He looked over at Pearl.

"We haven't been out to check anything yet," Pearl said. "That's the first thing we need to do." He twisted his mouth to one side and then relaxed it. "I doubt they'll bother with any brood mares. Clell, I think you and Flint better saddle up and go out to check on things. Get a full acount on everything, including mares and colts. Bring in all the stock that's been broke, and put it in the winter pasture." Pearl nodded towards the south. "Take your time and don't miss any. We don't want to say something's missin' if it ain't."

Clell had his lips pursed. He opened them and showed the pink toothless gums as he spoke. "You and Pete gonna go trail these bastards, then?"

Pearl wrinkled his nose and nodded. "That's what I'm thinkin'. We'll try to get Pete's stuff back first. I'll be back by nightfall or maybe tomorrow morning. By then we'll know where we are on head count, and if we come up short, then we'll go coyote huntin'."

Clell nodded with his mouth open.

Flint took a fierce pull on his cigarette. It was clear that he was all primed to hunt horse thieves, but it was also clear that Pearl's idea made the most sense.

Pearl spoke again. "Have you eaten yet, Pete?"

"No, I haven't, but I'm not hungry."

"Well, time's a-wastin'. Flint, how 'bout you help us catch up a couple of horses. Gypsy and Comet." Pearl looked at the old man. "Clell, if you could throw us together a little bag of grub, that'd be fine, too."

"Will do."

All four men got up from the table. Pete stood by as the other three pulled on boots and put on hats. Pearl and Flint each picked up ropes on the way out, and Pete followed them.

Pete climbed through the corral poles behind Flint, and right away he saw that the young man was a good hand at roping out horses. There were half a dozen head milling in the corral, and in less than a minute Flint had sailed his loop over the head of a blue roan.

"This one's Gypsy," he said to Pete. "Hold on to him, and I'll rope Comet for you." Flint reached over and took the rope that Pearl handed through the corral rails, and in another two minutes he was leading a solid brown horse out of the herd. "Pearl usually rides Gypsy," he said. "Let's put a halter on him, and I can take my rope back. Then I'll rope out a couple for me 'n' Clell."

Pearl opened the gate and they led the two horses out and over to the stable. Pearl slipped a halter onto Gypsy, loosened the rope and took it off, and handed it to Flint.

When it was just the two of them saddling the horses, Pearl said, "Got the girl, huh?"

Pete spoke over his shoulder as he looped the latigo through the cinch ring. "They sure did."

"Where'd you have her?"

"I had her in town for a few days, but she thought they were onto her, so we headed back out to the mountains. Camped about five miles from here. I guess I'm not so smart as I thought. They took her right out from under my nose while I was sleepin' in camp."

"Dirty bastards. I hope she's all right."

"So do I."

* * *

Pete led the way back to his camp, which was just as he had left it. After a quick once-over he rejoined Pearl, who had picked up the trail of the fugitives.

"Should be easy to follow," said the old horse trader. "Five or six head."

Pete nodded and looked at the sky. "I'd say they've got four hours on us. Maybe a little more." He spit out the stem of grass he had been chewing. "I doubt they're movin' very fast. They wouldn't expect me to get mounted again this soon."

Pearl spit off to the side. "We'll git 'em."

As they followed the trail, Pete mapped it all out in his mind. They weren't that far from the place where he had shot the two men or from the holding pen he had seen when Gregory walked up on him, but the trail didn't seem to be heading in that direction. Those places lay to the northwest, in the general direction of the rimrock camp he had shared with Rosy. The trail they were following went southwest, along the lower skirt of the mountains. That was close to the direction that Rosy thought they wanted to take her to begin with. Colorado.

Pete nodded as they rode on. It was probably the third man, with some new helper. It would take a couple of men to handle the horses as well as the girl.

They followed the trail for over two hours at a fairly good pace, with Pearl and Gypsy always a few yards ahead. At one place where the slope of the mountain leveled out, Pearl raised his hand and came to a halt. He swung down from the saddle, so Pete dismounted as well. Leading the horse, he walked forward to the place where Pearl was standing.

"Looks like they stopped for a rest here," he said.

Pete looked around at the open spot and saw where the grass had been mashed down. Off to the right were a few heaps of horse droppings. He led the horse forward and crouched by the flattened grass. "Looks like they sat here."

Pearl had come forward and had squatted also. His left arm rested on his knee with the hand on his bearded chin. He pointed with his right. "Yep. Here's a pair of bootheels. And here's another. And there's where they had yer gal sittin' between 'em."

Pete looked at him and nodded. Then he looked back at the ground. "No cigarette butts."

Pearl frowned and stood up, then walked over to the horse droppings. "Gettin' dry," he said. "Been a while." He turned around to Pete and winked. "But we're gainin' on 'em, I think."

They swung back into the saddle and pressed on. Always they moved south-southwest, farther from the Saddleback and the Black Diamond, closer to Colorado. The sun moved across the sky overhead. Twice they stopped to water the horses and roll a smoke. It was good weather for traveling, and the horses were making good time without wearing out.

The sun was starting to slip in the west when Pearl stopped his horse in the shade of a tall pine. He moved the reins to his right hand and pointed with his left. "Fresh," he said.

Pete looked down at the droppings. They were not steaming and slick, but they were not yet dry and crusted over. He nodded.

The two men rode on without a word for another hour. The shadows were stretching now, and the air was cooler. Pete figured they had less than two hours of daylight left. He knew they were covering ground faster than the other party was, and he hoped they caught up by nightfall. It not, he and Pearl were already agreed to sleep out in the open and move on in the morning.

Pearl stopped and waited for Pete to come up alongside. The old trail hand pushed back his hat and said in a low voice, "It's hard to tell, but I think we lost one horse out of this bunch."

Pete nodded, then whispered, "Hard to count tracks for sure in a bunch like this."

The older man said, "He might've gone off for somethin', or he might be off to the side, waitin' for us."

Pete nodded and pointed at his right eye, as if to say he'd be extra watchful.

Pearl settled his hat back on straight, nodded in return, and put his horse back on the trail.

Less than an hour later, when there was still

light but the sun had slipped beyond the mountain, Pearl stopped again. He lifted his head in signal, then wrinkled his nose and sniffed.

Pete rode up alongside and breathed in through his nose. Uh-huh. Woodsmoke.

Pearl winked at Pete and dismounted, then led his horse off the trail. Pete got down and followed. Pearl led the way through a stand of pines and then into a patch of aspens, which were leafless now. Pearl tied Gypsy to an aspen branch and pulled his rifle from the scabbard. When Pete had done the same, the two of them walked back out to the trail and continued to follow it.

After about a quarter of a mile, Pete heard a noise. It was a man's voice, sounding calm, not excited or happy. Pete stopped and made a signal with his tongue against the back of his teeth. Pearl stopped.

The sound was coming from a spot down to the left of the trail. There must be water there, Pete thought, because it wasn't at a good vantage point.

Pearl led the way and Pete followed, the two of them stepping softly and pointing their rifles downward. Their way led them through pines and into aspens with low-lying junipers. After a hundred yards, Pete could see color and movement through the trees. They both dropped to a crouch. The camp was about sixty yards away, but they could see nothing of it.

Pearl took off his hat and set it on the ground.

Pete did the same. Then Pearl, still in a crouch but with his haunches up off his heels, began to duck-walk forward. Pete did likewise.

Twenty yards farther, Pete began to pick out words. Another ten yards, and he could identify phrases. He thought he knew the voice, but he raised his head to make sure. The man's back was turned and he was wearing a long drover's coat, but Pete knew him for sure by the round, narrow-brimmed hat that looked like the tip of a bullet. It was Chicago Thorne.

Pete hunkered back down, and with his left ear to the campsite he looked at Pearl. The older man made a tiny frown and cocked his head as if to say, "Let's listen." Then Pete, without uttering a sound, mouthed the information to his partner: "Thorne."

Pearl nodded and shifted into a sitting position.

Pete settled onto his knees and rested his rifle in the crook of his arm. He could hear Thorne's voice pretty well, but Rosy's was barely distinguishable.

"Just you and me. Don't you like that?"

Something garbled.

"He went back to put your lover boy on ice. Probably won't be back till late tonight or early in the morning."

Rosy's voice came through garbled again, and Thorne said something in a low voice. Pearl motioned with his head, pushed into a crouch, and led the way through the brush for another ten yards. When he and Pete stopped, the voices came through clearly.

Rosy's voice had a challenging tone to it. "What makes you think I would do that?"

"You probably gave some to Garnett last night in that tent."

"You must be crazy." She pronounced it with a hard *s*.

"He's a regular little whore-hound. Why wouldn't he?"

Pete felt himself wince as he heard Rosy's voice again.

"I don't care about that, or what he does. But I don't do it."

"Oh, hell. Don't give me that. It's written all over you."

"That's just what you think. But you're wasting your time. You should be thinking about where to sell these horses. I can help you more there."

"Is that right?"

"Sure I can. Mr. Burr told me all about it."

"You make me laugh. I know ten times as much about all of this as he ever would."

"Then you must know who the King is."

"Don't you worry about what I know or don't know. You're a smart little Mexican, aren't you?"

"Not as smart as you think you are."

"I meant smart-aleck."

Pete raised up enough to get a look. Thorne was still standing with his back to him, looking across the fire at Rosy, who was seated on a log or stump. Pete settled back down.

Thorne's voice carried over again. "It's goin' to be another cold night."

"I don't care."

"You ought to. It can get pretty cold unless someone lets you under the blankets."

"I already told you."

"Suit yourself. But if you can give it to someone like Garnett, you can give it to me."

"I already told you, he doesn't mean anything to me."

Pete flinched. Then he heard Thorne's voice again.

"That's not the point. The point is, whether you're goin' to give it to me nice or not."

"And if I don't?"

"Suit yourself. Like I said, there's just the two of us."

Pete had heard enough. His mouth was dry and he could feel himself shaking, but he knew it was time to step in. He looked at Pearl, then pointed at himself and toward the campsite. Pearl nodded.

Pete stood up and snicked a shell into the chamber of his rifle. "Hold it right there, Thorne," he called out.

Thorne stood without moving, his back towards Pete. Then he edged to his left around the campfire.

Pete, meanwhile, was moving forward and to his right, away from Pearl. By now he had located the horses, on the other side of the camp. If he had to shoot, Rosy and the horses would be out of the line of fire.

Thorne continued to move to his left, and as he did he brought something into view that made Pete stop short. He held a lever-action rifle at his hips, with the muzzle pointed at Rosy. He had his thumb on the hammer and his finger on the trigger. Light was fading now, and the firelight reflected off the rifle and off of Thorne's black leather vest.

"Maybe you heard what I told her," he said, "but I'll repeat it to you. Suit yourself."

From the corner of his eye, Pete could see Pearl getting into position. Thorne did not seem to notice, as he kept his gaze locked on Pete.

Pete shook his head. "We'll have it your way, Chicago."

"You're gettin' smarter, Garnett. You just take your rifle by the barrel end, and hold it up like a dead chicken, and carry it over here and set it down. Be careful. I don't want it to go off."

Pete did as he was told, turning the gun up and away from him, holding it up to clear the brush. As he did so, he watched Thorne's right hand. The thumb came off the hammer, and the finger came out of the trigger guard.

Suddenly the air *whoofed* against Garnett as Thorne lurched backwards, and the deafening crash of Pearl's rifle shattered the cool mountain air.

Rosy fell to the ground and screamed, and

Pete brought the rifle back around into position as he charged forward.

Thorne was laid out flat, and his rifle was on the ground ten yards away. His right hand was on his chest.

Pete stopped at the campfire. Rosy was covering her face and crouching. "Are you all right?" he asked.

She looked up, terror in the dark eyes, and nodded.

Pete walked around the campfire and looked down at Thorne. The left hand rose in the air and settled by the right. Blood was seeping up through the black leather vest, staining the right hand and now the left, those trim hands that would never wind a watch again.

Pete turned to Rosy. "Do you know this man?"

She shook her head.

"Then he's not the third man. The one with the horses."

"No. The other one was."

"The one that went back to get me?"

"Yes. That one."

Chapter Thirteen

For as much as Pete respected Pearl, he wondered if the old horse trader hadn't been too quick on the trigger. Another man was dead, and even if that part was unavoidable, there was a practical side to it. Chicago Thorne obviously knew who the King was, and now there was no way to get it out of him. Furthermore, Pete was left to wonder if Thorne's description of Grant was bogus. It most probably was, but anything Chicago Thorne ever knew was now locked away.

As for Pearl, he sounded just as firm as he did the day Pete told him about the first shooting. He seemed satisfied with having dispatched Thorne with one shot and getting Pete's horses back. To Pete, the older man seemed like a stern avenger, since the horse stealing in this case was obviously part of a personal vendetta and not just an act of horse thievery in itself. Pearl, however, repeated his earlier line: "We can't let the sons of bitches run all over us." He spoke as if he, too, had been plundered, but as of that moment neither he nor Pete knew. Nor did he seem remorseful on a personal level. He said, "There's one of 'em out of business, that's for damn sure. When the other one comes back, we can take care of him."

The raid on Pete's camp had clearly been calculated, since Thorne had brought an extra saddled horse from the Saddleback. That told Pete that the men had planned foremost to get their hands on Rosy and that taking the horses was secondary, to leave him on foot as much as anything else.

Pearl's idea was for Pete and Rosy to ride back to their camp and turn the Saddleback horses loose to drift back to their own range. He could take Comet back to his place and check on his own stock, and Pete and Rosy could meet up with him the next day. Night was coming on, and that meant they would be riding off in the dark in two different directions. As they talked it over, Pearl's idea seemed just as safe as any other plan and probably safer than spending the night nearby.

"We should have some moonlight to travel by," Pete added. "It was a bright half-moon last night."

"Well, let's do it that way," said Pearl.

Just before they split up, it occurred to Pete that he could check the holding pen in the morning. He told Pearl what he was thinking, and the horse trader agreed it was a good idea. "If there's any horses of mine, bring 'em along, of course."

"You bet I will."

Then it was off into the dusk—Pearl with his two horses, Pete and Rosy with their three plus the two Saddleback horses. Pearl moved out as Pete helped Rosy into her saddle. Pete checked his cinch before mounting up, and as he did so he glanced back in the direction where Chicago Thorne was lying dead. It was a bum deal, he thought. Chicago wasn't all bad. He just made a few wrong choices and probably thought a little too highly of his chances of getting away with it all. Pete looked at the vanishing figure of Pearl on Gypsy, leading Comet. The old horse trader probably wasn't very worried about Thorne. To him, it was just one more down.

Pete swung aboard and looked over at Rosy, who was sitting in the saddle and pulling on her wool gloves. She was most likely trying not to think about it. With good reason, he thought.

She didn't know the man Thorne, and neither did Pearl, to any extent. Pete shook his head. It was too bad. You rode for the same outfit with a man, you bunked and ate with him, and then you found out he was like a rattlesnake in your bedroll. It hadn't come as a great surprise, but the way it ended left Pete troubled. Even if Thorne sneered at both Pete and Pearl, which he seemed to do, and even if had something in mind for Rosy, there should have been a better way.

Rosy looked over and smiled.

Pete nodded and smiled back. "How do you say *ready*?"

"*Listo*," she said.

"Least-o," he repeated, and then they moved out into the dusk.

Pete figured it was well past midnight by the time they found their campsite. He made quick work of staking out Star and the two leased horses, and he stripped the gear from the two Saddleback horses. They would probably stay near the other horses at least until daylight. As for the company saddles, bridles, and blankets, he decided he would hang those things in a tree and then pick them up later when he had a chance. He thought of storing them at Pearl's, but that would require leading the horses there. He imagined Pearl wouldn't want the gear or the horses that close to his place.

With Rosy's help he rolled out the bedding. He decided against setting up the tent, since it would be for only a few hours and he didn't want anything screening out the sounds. Then he had an idea. He decided to set up the tent where it had been before and to move the bed to a new spot thirty yards away. That seemed like a good precaution.

When he awoke in the morning, everything was in place. Rosy was still asleep, and it gave him a good feeling to hear her soft, regular breathing. From where he lay he could see all five horses in the grey light, and by lifting his head he could see the bleak shape of the tent. At that moment he also noticed that the blanket had a layer of frost on it.

Pete rolled out of the blankets, thinking he might as well get a start on the day. Whoever the third man was, he might come calling. Pete imagined he had come by this way, found no one, and returned to the rendezvous spot with Thorne. It wouldn't be long until he rounded up another partner or two and went back at it. Pete could not picture the man with any detail. He had asked Rosy again about the leather thong, and she had said he was wearing a handkerchief. So when Pete imagined the man, it was a faceless form that came to mind. Rosy could still put a face on him, though, so he wasn't likely to give up at this point.

As Pete stood up to settle into his boots, he looked down at the bed on the ground. Rosy's dark hair was visible, but her face was under the covers. She could sleep a little longer. He noticed the frost again and realized he could have used the canvas manty for a top sheet.

He moved quietly as he went about the chores of starting a fire, fetching water, and taking the horses to the stream. When he got back with the horses, Rosy was standing by the fire and combing her hair. She was still in her outdoor clothes, which didn't set off her figure very well, but Pete enjoyed seeing her and sharing the camp with her.

The kettle of water sat against the coals as they had their biscuits and coffee. Pete noticed again her dark lashes and dark eyes, the honey skin, and the white cord that held the crucifix. The physical details were becoming more familiar to him; he was seeing them as things that he knew, things that were part of his own world now. He hoped she saw him that way, too, but something he had heard the day before came back to bother him.

"I've got a question," he said.

"Yes?"

"You know, Pearl and I overheard a little of the talk between you and that fella Thorne before we cut in yesterday."

Rosy had her gloved hands around the can of hot coffee, and she lowered the can from her lips as she nodded.

"Well, there was this one thing that bothered me."

"You mean what he said about you and the *putillas*?"

"Well, no, I didn't like that either, but I mean something else. Something you said."

"What was that?"

"It was the part where you said I didn't mean anything to you."

Her face took on a sad look. "I had to tell him that. He thought we—you know, did something."

Pete looked down at the ashes at the edge of the fire. "Yeah, but it went further than that." He looked back up at her. "I thought that maybe you did care a little. I mean, you did kiss me back there in town."

Rosy's face softened. "Yes, I did, and I do care. But I couldn't tell him I liked you. In the first place it would just make him jealous, and then he would think we did something."

"Then you didn't mean it. The part about my not meaning anything."

She smiled. "How could I mean it if I kissed you? That's not something we do just like that."

Pete smiled back. He looked at her lovely neck and the white cord, and then his eyes met hers again. "Then you're not put out about what he said about me and the—those other women?"

"No," she said. Her eyes were soft as she looked at him. "You and I talked about that. You said it was in the past."

"And it is," he said, "as far as you and I are concerned. You mean somethin' to me, and if I want to mean somethin' to you, that's the only way it can be."

"Well," she said, "he was just trying to get

something he wanted, and he thought you and I, you know . . ."

"Did something."

"Yes."

"Well, we didn't, and that's all fine." He looked at the fire, and another thought crossed his mind. It must have shown on his face.

"What's the matter?" she asked.

"You didn't really know anything about Burr and the horses, did you?"

She laughed. "No. I was just trying to change the subject when I told him that."

"I know it sounded stupid to ask, but I don't like to carry these things around inside."

"That's fine."

Pete noticed the first bubbles forming on the grey enamel of the inside of the kettle, down where the kettle touched the coals. He leaned forward and dipped two fingers in the water. "It's gettin' warm," he said. "See what you think."

She set her coffee on the ground, slipped off her right glove, leaned over, and tested the water. "That's good."

He lifted the kettle by the bail handle, which was still not hot, and stood up to carry the water to a clear, flat spot away from the fire. She stood up also and set her gloves on the rock she had been sitting on. Then she stood facing Pete over the kettle of warm water.

"Thank you," she said.

He nodded. Then he leaned forward to kiss

her, and her lips met his for an instant. As they drew apart, he laughed a short, nervous laugh. "We'd better be careful we don't spill the water."

She gave him a broad smile, and her whole face lit up. "We'll be careful," she said.

He turned away to go about the tasks of breaking camp. Everything seemed all right between them.

As they rode towards the spot where Pete had seen the holding pen, he wondered what they might find there. He wasn't sure that he would know all of Pearl's stock. Pete knew the brand, a teepee made out of half an X on top of a triangle, but not all of Pearl's horses carried it. As a general practice, Pearl branded the horses he raised as well as any unbranded horses that came into his hands. He kept papers on any branded horses he bought or acquired through trade, and at a given time he could have horses with any number of brands on them. Pete decided he would deliver anything with Pearl's teepee brand, and he would turn loose anything else.

When they reached the holding pen, which was less than an hour's ride after breaking camp, Pete left Rosy with their horses while he went into the trees. There were six horses in the pen, and Pete knew every one of them. They were from the Saddleback, top horses from the herd Dusty had turned out to winter range. Pete shook his head. Stealing from the company—

and yet, Thorne could just as easily have put Dusty's horse Chub in the bunch, and he didn't. As Pete let down the rails to turn the horses loose, he thought, that's where Thorne must have drawn the line—between stealing from the company and stealing from a fellow cowhand. True, he had taken Star, but he wasn't working on his own then, and it had been part of a different plan.

The horses did not linger but went straight up the canyon. Pete imagined they had not had water for a day and a half and had a good memory of where that had been. The other two Saddleback horses, which had trailed along free behind Pete and Rosy and the packhorse, went trotting after the herd as Pete stepped out of the trees.

Pete told Rosy what he had found. Then he said, "If I had time I'd like to wreck that pen. Or burn it. But I think we'd better get goin' and ride for the Flat Rock."

The three of them stood outside Pearl's cabin in the sunshine as Pete told his story, including an explanation of how Thorne had been the only one staying at the Saddleback.

Pearl listened and nodded. "Makes sense," he said. "Start where it's easiest, where people are least likely to notice. I imagine he was plannin' to go back there and draw wages, too."

"Probably," Pete said. "He didn't have all his gear with him."

Pearl spit on the ground and then looked at Rosy. "Excuse me," he said.

Pete imagined Pearl was not used to having women around. "Where's Flint and Clell?" he asked.

"They're out checkin' on things. There was only a couple of head they couldn't account for yesterday, and those wouldn't be a first choice for a horse rustler, so the boys went to take a closer look."

"Sounds like you were right, then. If they were goin' to hit your herd at all, they were probably going to do it towards the end."

"They still might," said Pearl. "This ain't over just because we put one of 'em under. It might be just gettin' started."

"Where does it end, Pearl?"

"With the King, I'd say."

"We don't even know who he is. We have to work our way up to him. Get someone that'll talk."

Pearl raised his eyebrows and seemed to catch the message. "Probably so. Personally, I like to shoot first and ask questions later, but I see what you mean. We need to catch a bird that'll sing."

"The question is, how do we do that?"

Pearl shrugged. "Either catch 'em in the act or let 'em come to us."

Pete scraped his upper teeth on his lower lip as he ran through his thought. Then he said, "Maybe I shouldn't have let those horses loose.

But I figured they'd been in there at least a day and a half without water."

Pearl made a sucking sound in the corner of his mouth. "Nah, you did right. After we put that one bird down, the others'll be a couple of days gettin' things back in order. There's probably nobody even gonna check on those horses for a day or two. If we'd found the horses first, then we could have waited to see who dropped in. But as it was, you did right. Those horses needed to get to water, and it un-did things the rest of the way for these fellas. We just have to wait for their next move and see what we can turn up then."

"I tell you, Pearl, I've got this gut feeling that Flagg's man Gregory is the one we missed yesterday and the one that got away when I had it out with those other two." He looked at Rosy and nodded once.

Pearl looked at Pete. "You think so? You see, I don't even know the man."

"Rosy doesn't either, at least by name. But I've met him a couple of times. He's hard as a rock, I know that. I don't know how much we could get out of him, though."

"Can't get blood out of a stone, they say. Or water either, for that matter. I suppose it's the same with Flagg." Pearl stuck out his lower lip. "Does he have anyone else workin' for him?"

"Not that I know of." Then an image crossed Pete's mind. "But there is another person I could possibly ask."

"Who's that?"

Pete glanced at Rosy and back at Pearl. "Flagg's wife."

Pearl raised his eyebrows. "Do you know her?"

"I've talked to her, and I think I could again. But I can't just ride up to their door."

Pearl shook his head. "No, not if Flagg's in this thing at all. He and what's-his-name might just as soon shoot you on sight."

"So far they've been all smiles, but that could change. And I agree with you."

Pearl winced. "Then how do we get to her?"

Pete reached for his cigarette makings. "We might be able to send a messenger."

The horse trader looked at Rosy and back at Pete. "Who?"

"What do you think of Flint?"

"He's got the guts for it, but you never know if he'll say what he's supposed to and keep his mouth shut otherwise."

Pete handed the tobacco to Pearl. "We'll let him carry a letter. He can't foul that up."

Pearl laughed. "He sure can't." Then he turned to Rosy. "Well, miss," he said, "it sounds like we won't have to send you." He handed the tobacco back to Pete. "Let's put these horses away first, and then we'll roll us a smoke and get into the letter-writin' business."

They decided not to put any names on the page—not in the greeting, or in a signature, or in any references. After a few runs at it, Pete had a clean copy that looked like it would work:

Not long ago I had a drink of brandy with a lady. She told me not to be afraid to see her again. If it could be arranged I would like to speak with her.

"That's about as good as you're gonna get it," Pearl said. "That word 'speak' hits the right note. Better than 'talk,' the way you had it. Sounds just right."

"Good." Pete folded the letter in half and then in half again.

When Flint and Clell came in for noonday dinner, Pearl told the young man of his errand and gave him his instructions.

"You put this in your hat, and you don't show it to no one but this Logan Gregory. You know Flagg, don't you? Well, be damn sure he doesn't get it, and if you run into him, don't say anything about Pete. You just find Gregory and give him this note, tell him who it's from, and he'll probably write something for you to bring back. You got all that?"

"Yeah, I got it." Flint seemed sullen at being talked down to, and he glanced more than once at Rosy, but it was clear that he knew he was being sent on an important mission.

"Well, good enough, then. Get back as soon as you can, but don't run your horse into the ground."

Flint settled the pinched brown hat onto his head. "I'll do 'er," he said.

Flint was back before dark. He put his horse away, then came back to the cabin, where Pete, Rosy, and Pearl were standing outside. Clell was lying down inside. Flint took off his hat, and with the first two fingers of his right hand he drew out a folded piece of paper which he handed to Pete.

The response was written in a neat cursive hand, also with no personal references. Pete scanned the letter and looked up at Flint.

"He wrote this while you were there?"

Flint bobbed his head up and down. "You bet. Right on the spot."

"You're sure it was Gregory?"

"Just like you described him. About my height, clean-shaven, thinks he's the cock of the walk. Talks like a preacher. Even had the leather whang around his neck."

Pete nodded and read the note again, more carefully. It was the type of letter he would expect the gatekeeper to write:

The lady of whom you speak, or write, will be at home for your visit tomorrow at ten a.m. It shall be contrived that no impediments be present.

Pete handed the letter to Rosy, who read it and passed it on to Pearl. He read it and looked at Pete.

"That means the coast is clear."

"Uh-huh."

Pearl handed the letter back to Pete, and as he did so he looked at Flint. "How about the letter Pete wrote?"

Flint pointed at his own throat. "Gone. I ate it."

Chapter Fourteen

If ever he felt that he was riding into enemy territory, Pete felt it as he rode down into the Black Diamond headquarters. He knew that if he ran into Flagg he could say he dropped in by way of open invitaiton, but he also knew it would be a rather naked lie. What he would meet at the ranch house depended on Gregory, whose allegiance to Flagg and the Mrs. seemed to work like a pendulum. From the circumstances, Pete guessed that Gregory's primary loyalty was to the Mrs. But from the way the hired man had thumbed his own chest at the end of the last visit, Pete supposed that there would be times, moments at least, in which Gregory's self-interest let the pendulum swing the other way.

Today was probably not such a time, he

thought, or he would have been intercepted by now. If Gregory had turned coat, Flagg would probably not let Pete come all the way to head-quarters when he had miles of open country for a meeting. Unless he wanted to stage a scene to embarrass his wife—no, thought Pete, he wouldn't do that with Gregory around.

His questions were answered when the door opened without his knocking. Lenore, wearing a white dress, made a bright and almost daz-zling appearance in the daylight.

"Come on in," she said as she led the way into the sitting room. "Please have a seat."

Pete took off his hat and sat down in the same chair as before.

"Relax," she said. "Logan diverted the master. Convinced him that there were rustlers at work out there and that they should go take a look."

Probably took him on a wild goose chase after me. "Thank you for letting me come today."

"I'm glad you felt free to ask," she said.

Pete thought she smiled in a comforting, cozy way. He had noticed her trim figure again as he walked into the room behind her, and there was a magnetism in the air as there had been during his last visit. On his ride over he had prepared himself to resist temptations, and now that he was here, he felt again that there was not as much temptation as there was enjoyment of the moment. It was as if he was in a warm bath and she was in another tub next to his. He also knew, as he had known before, that she had the power to change the tone of the visit if she wanted.

Yet he trusted her. In their last visit she had shared morsels of confidence with him that she could not share with her husband or lover. He felt that confidence again, and he felt that it was valuable in and for itself. Some of that confidence had been about Gregory, with whom she no doubt had a separate kind of confidence. Pete knew, almost by instinct, that if he and the Mrs. sported at this point, they would lose that good feeling they both wanted to maintain.

"May I offer you something? Coffee?"

"Sure. Coffee sounds fine."

"Do you take anything with it?"

"Sugar, if you have it."

"I'll be back in a minute." She got up and left the room. Her dress fit her very much like the previous one did. It did not hug her figure, but it showed it to advantage.

She came back into the room with a tray. On it were two cups and saucers and a sugar bowl, all of matching pale-white china. The cups were full of coffee, and a silver spoon lay next to the sugar bowl. She set the tray on a chair that was midway between Pete's chair and the sofa but off to one side. As she set the tray down, Pete noticed a ring on her left hand. It had a green stone, which he imagined was emerald. The stone was rectangular with beveled corners and edges, and it sat in a casket-like setting of little gold bars. Lenore turned to Pete and smiled, and he noticed she was wearing a matching green pendant that hung from a delicate gold chain. The pendant looked octagonal, with facets to take off the points and edges. It was beautiful jewelry that she wore, bright but not large, and it made a nice match with her green eyes.

"Help yourself," she said. She took one cup and saucer and returned to the sofa.

Pete added a spoonful of sugar to his coffee, stirred it, and sat back in his chair.

Lenore looked at him and gave him a reassuring nod.

Pete took a sip of coffee, then a deep breath, and began. "I remember you told me last time that you don't know much about your husband's business doin's."

"That's right. He keeps it that way, and it's just as well for me."

"Uh-huh. I don't want to seem like I'm prying, but I'm trying to find out some information that might help me with some trouble I'm having."

Her face showed an open expression. "The possible trouble I spoke of last time?"

"It might be related. I don't want to tell you anything you'd just as soon not know, so I'll put it this way. Do you know anything about a man named Grant?"

Her face seemed to shrink. "Well . . . yes. I should say I do. It was his name before he changed it to Flagg."

Pete was surprised at his own reaction, surprised that he took it so calmly and was not stunned. It was like a moment in a dream, seeing something that he knew but that he had not realized he knew. It was like opening a room and seeing a strange figure in jewels and robes but recognizing the face. Flagg was the King.

"He changed his name?"

"Yes. It used to be Grant. Rex Grant. After the trouble in Colorado, when he wanted to leave and make a new start, he said he wanted a new name. He said I had caused him too much shame. For all I know, it had something to do with his business dealings, but that's the face he put on it with me."

Pete gave a low whistle. "Is that when he grew the beard?"

"Yes. He didn't have it before."

Pete sat silent. Was there a good way to tell a woman that her husband was a horse thief and murderer and that her lover was probably in it up to his elbows? She might already know the part about the husband, or she might be glad to learn it for its possible value to her. But the other part could cause trouble.

Pete recalled a piece of advice he had gotten from Pearl while they waited for Flint to come back from his errand. Pearl said, "Don't tell any more than you have to—not to anyone." Now, as he sat in the parlor with Lenore the Mrs., he thought he should tell her something. After all, she hadn't held out on him, and it wouldn't seem right if he did that to her.

He cleared his throat. "I think I should tell you why I asked."

She nodded as if to say, "Go ahead."

"There's been a little trouble with horses disappearing, and there's been mention of a man behind it that nobody knows. But they call him Grant."

"That doesn't surprise me."

"It could be that Flagg, or men that know him, round up the horses and Grant sells them. Then someone tries to trace it back here, and no one knows him."

"That could be. He was Grant in Colorado, and he goes there on occasion, as you know."

Pete hesitated. "I don't know if your hired man might be mixed up in it."

Lenore sipped her coffee and set the cup and saucer on her lap. "Logan tells me he knows how to keep his hands clean."

"Let's hope so," Pete answered. Then he thought, *Of course. The third man. Lets others take the bullet.* He lifted his head slightly to get her attention, and then he said, "Have you heard any mention of a man named Chicago Thorne?"

She shook her head. "No. Not at all. I would remember a name like that."

"How about Tucker?"

Her green eyes came up. "That was Mace's last name."

It was like the dream again. The two faces, five years apart. That was what he had seen before, without knowing it. The sitting room came back into focus as he found his voice. "The man I shot. Was there another one?"

"Yes, he had a brother who came here to work for a while. But he didn't stay long."

"Was he one of those that just up and left?"

"Yes, he and a partner of his, a man called Palmer."

Pete nodded.

"You seem to be adding things up."

"Puttin' two and two together, that's for sure." He looked her in the eyes. "There's some men been killed. And I think your husband has got more against me than just that business from before." Pete had an image of Gregory at that moment also, but he said nothing.

Lenore's eyebrows tightened. "I think it would be best for all of us if he had to answer for at least some of it."

"I think so, too. I just wish I knew the best way of bringin' it about."

Her thoughts seemed to turn inward. "I'll talk to Logan about it," she said. "Don't be surprised if we ask you to help again, after all."

Pete took a deep breath. "All right. But I'll ask you to do me one favor."

"What's that?"

"Don't tell him I asked you about any names."

"What names?" She was smiling again, in the good way.

Pete smiled back. They were in their two tubs again.

*　　*　　*

On his way back to the Flat Rock, Pete had time to absorb what he had learned in his visit with Lenore. No wonder she didn't like being called Mrs. Flagg. And she probably hadn't minded dropping the name Grant.

His thoughts went back to Chicago Thorne. As soon as Thorne's guilt had become evident, Pete had suspected that the description of Grant was counterfeit. He had thought that Grant might be just a shadow figure, a name with no face. Now he had both, and he could see to what extent Thorne had been mocking him.

As for Gregory, Pete was sure he was the wolf in the thicket. Pete hadn't seen him, but Rosy had—twice. Unless the gatekeeper left the country damn soon with the Mrs., he would have reason to want to close Rosy's mouth.

The one with the most reason to make a move, of course, was Flagg himself. The King. He was the big danger, and he probably wouldn't try to put on a friendly guise for much longer.

Pete took a long, deep breath. It had all come together, after all this time lost on names and puzzles. He had taken everything at face value, and yet the truth had not been so very far beneath the surface. The King was a bigger danger than he had realized, but at least now he knew. Knowledge took some of the fear out of it.

Thorne, Gregory, the King—they all treated

him like a dummy. Maybe they were all smarter than he was. That was all right. Plenty of people were. But he knew what he knew, and that included things that each of the others, even the Mrs., did not know.

He was in it up to his neck, but at least he knew how and how deep. That was more than he could say about Gregory, who thought he was his own master.

Good enough. Now it was a matter of how to get out—if he could.

Pete shared his knowledge with Pearl and Rosy, including the part about Logan Gregory's probable relation to the Mrs. but not including the part about the Edwards Hotel and his first encounter with the lady. That part seemed too tangled for the present moment. He simplified it by saying that Gregory and the Mrs. had earlier information that they could bring up and that could put an additional squeeze on the King.

Pearl blew a cloud of smoke out through his nostrils. "It would be a good turn in the game if they went to the law and peached on him."

Pete studied the ash on his own cigarette. "Gregory might be in too deep. The King could bring him down with him."

"Yeah."

Pete looked at Rosy. "If Gregory can get him locked up or out of the way and then skip the country, that would be the best. Otherwise, we're up against both of 'em all the way."

Rosy looked at Pete, who sat at her side, and at Pearl at the end of the table.

Pearl pushed back his hat and scratched the side of his head. "How long till your pilgrims show up?"

"Three days. I'd sure like to have this wrapped up before I take out a party of tenderfeet."

Pearl looked at Rosy. "We need to keep you safe. That's number one." He looked at Pete. "You know, I'm not a quick one to go to the law, even less so than you are, but if somethin' doesn't break in a couple of days, maybe I'll have to." He looked back at Rosy. "If I do, we're gonna need you all the way."

"That's fine."

Pearl lifted his eyebrows. "Let's try this for an idea. Pete, you get this girl out of the way for two days. Go up on top where you said you were before, on the other side. I'll keep an eye on things here. They don't know I'm the one that got the drop on Thorne, so they won't come after me directly, though naturally they know I'm thick with you. I'll keep my eyes and ears open. If nothin' breaks in two days, then I'll go to the law and then we'll come and find you."

Pete looked at Rosy and she nodded. He looked back at Pearl. "That sounds all right. We can leave right away and be there in time to set camp before dark."

Pearl nodded as he fingered his beard. "Let

me get Flint, and we'll ride with you at least part of the way."

All the way up the mountain, Pete watched the sky as well as the surrounding terrain. They had had a light snow, and now it looked as if a bigger snow was on the way. Pearl agreed, and Flint put in his opinion as well.

"Big storm," he said. "I knew it was gonna be an early winter."

Pearl and Flint turned back at timberline, while Pete and Rosy and the packhorse went on up and over. They set their camp near the place where Pete had camped by himself. With the tent pitched, firewood stacked, and the horses staked out, Pete saw that they still had an hour before sundown.

"Let me show you a place I found when I was here last," he said.

Rosy looked at him. "What kind of place?"

"Just a place to sit."

Together they walked across a rocky mountainside. Pete took her hand from time to time when the trail was steep, and occasionally they paused to look around. Game trails crisscrossed through the sagebrush and dry grass. Here and there on the slope could be seen a lone pine or cedar, but the trees did not get thick until a ways below them. Pete could see the spot he was headed for up ahead. It looked like one large cedar, but he knew it was actually a small ring of cedars that formed a cove.

When they reached the cedars they turned and looked outward. The world spread away from them on all sides, so that Pete had the feeling they were on top of the world and had it all to themselves. Throughout the afternoon the clouds had been thickening, but now the sun had slipped low enough to flood the scene with rich golden light.

"It's beautiful," said Rosy. "The land, and the color of the light."

"It sure is. It's the clouds that give it that color."

They stood there for a few moments, saying nothing, until Pete motioned toward the ring of cedars. He heard her intake of breath.

"You see," he said, "from a distance it looks like one big tree. But there are—count them—seven."

The ground sloped down from the back of the cove toward the opening where they stood. Across the middle was a flat spot, a sort of bench, where deer or elk or maybe even another person had rested in shelter. Pete took her by the hand and led her in to sit down. They faced the sun, which was on its way to setting beyond the westward mountains. They could not see the rest of the mountain at their back, and although the distant mountains might be higher, the sense of elevation was supreme.

"It's like we're on top of the world," he said. "Right here on our throne."

"Yes," she said. "It's so pretty."

He knew in that moment that he must kiss her. She must have known it too, for she turned to him as he moved to put his left arm around her. He closed his eyes as their lips met, and then he was lost in the moist freedom of their kiss—floating out over the canyons on the golden air.

They drew apart and looked into each other's eyes. Then they moved together again, more briefly now, and when they separated they re-clined together—he on his left side and she on her right—on the thin grass of the sloping earth.

They kissed again, and moved and teetered and swayed. Then she was on her back, and he was lying with his left side on the ground and his right side on her. He moved a little to his right and they met again, squirming slowly as the kiss surged and faded. He had the sense of being here on this piece of earth, with his back to the open world and sky that stretched away, and he also had the sense of the two of them, clasped as one, floating in the amber sky.

She was gasping now, almost crying, as she moved to her left and out from under him.

He looked into her face, damp with perspiration, and he felt the heat of his own body. He also felt what he couldn't tell her, the dampness of his own release.

"We can't," she said.

"It's all right," he answered. "I'm sorry."

"Don't be sorry. But we just can't do any more."

"I know."

"That's for marriage."

"I know. I understand."

That evening, as they sat by the fire and waited for the kettle of water to heat, Rosy said, "That boy needs to take a bath."

"Who? Flint?"

"Yes."

"He sure does." Then Pete thought back and realized it had been over a week since he himself had had a bath. "Wouldn't do me any harm either," he said.

"I didn't mean it that way."

"But it's true." He felt the stubble on his beard. "And a shave, too."

When the water was warm he set it inside the tent for her. A little while later she called to him, and he took the water away and pitched it. She said she would stay in the tent, so he was left to himself to heat a second kettle and get cleaned up.

While the water was heating, he took off his boots and socks. Usually he didn't worry about any of this until he got to a stream in warm weather or back to the bunkhouse or into town. In cold weather a fellow didn't sweat all that much anyway, and maybe after a week he had to scrub his underside with snow, but the rest could usually wait. Now, however, he was disgusted with his own accumulations. He dug the lint and grime from between his toes, then used his clasp knife to trim his toenails and finger-nails. He soaped his face and neck and shaved in the dark, feeling for the spots he missed and going over them. Then he carried the kettle away from the campsite and bathed in the cold mountain air, pouring the last of the water down his front and back.

He dried off with a cloth sack. It actually wasn't that cold. Not with the cloud cover. It was going to snow again. That was good. If they stayed put, they could see if anyone else came by. They had everything they needed—food and shelter, ammunition and horses. It felt good up on top here. He hoped the King and Gregory were down at the Black Diamond and stayed there. Better yet, he hoped that Gregory and the Mrs. were planning to put the King on ice, to use Thorne's phrase. It was a cold way to look at it, but that would be best. Best of luck to you, Lenore.

Rosy was asleep when he went into the tent. She smelled clean and warm again as he crawled under the covers. He felt clean, too. It was some trouble to clean up out here, but he was glad he did. It felt good to be clean.

He lay on his side and put his hand on her waist. Such a good girl. He could have feeling for a woman again, he knew that. It was already there, like a clear mountain spring.

A light breeze rippled the tent. It was a good

tent. Setting the bed to one side of the center pole put his back against the canvas. That wouldn't be good if they got snow. He could move. Better to get snow. Come a big snow.

The King

Send a boy out to do a man's job. Probably had his finger in the pie and they walked right up on him. All that for nothing.

Should have killed the pup when I had him in the sights. No—better now after all, now that he's got the girl with him again. Put him on the meathook and then see how she can wiggle. Long time since I had me a dark one.

They say it really quivers if you hold a gun to their head. Under the jaw, maybe. Then make my sword a ploughshare.

Chapter Fifteen

In the morning the world was white. Pete looked out of the tent onto a snowfall of six to eight inches. It was reassuring, the quiet softness that a good snow brought. He knew it would make for some difficulty in finding firewood and for the horses finding graze, and he knew that two or three snows with freezing in between could make everything a struggle. But a good snow like this, all by itself, muffled the world and made it serene.

The timing was good, too, he thought. The snow covered any tracks that were legible from their coming up the day before, and it would require any new travelers or visitors to sign in.

Pete scraped the snow to one side of the fire pit, then brought out dry firewood he had cached the night before. He got a blaze going and began to melt snow for coffee water. It was a tedious process, adding snow and adding snow, but it was pleasant all the same. He had a coffeepot now, so he could use a can to scoop snow and fill the pot, wait for the snow to melt, and then scoop in more.

While the water was heating he went to check on the horses. They smelled rich in the clean air, and they were doing well at pawing down to the grass. They also had sagebrush on their breaths, so he knew they were getting by well enough. Snow had iced up along the ridges of their backs, so he brushed off most of it with his leather-gloved hand as he spoke to each horse. Then he went back to camp.

Rosy was up and standing by the fire. She brushed a wisp of hair off her cheek as he walked up. Her dark hair and dark features looked sharp and pretty in this world of white.

"What do you think of the snow?" he asked.

She smiled and her eyes sparkled. "It's beautiful."

Pete turned and looked at the surroundings, a continuous blanket of unbroken snow except for the trail he had made to check the horses. "It sure is," he said. He took a broader look around. From here to the crest it was mostly treeless and white. Below them, beyond the horses, the dark evergreens rose up out of whiteness, their branches sprinkled with the snow that held there. Off in the distance, the shaggy dark mountains looked powdered.

He looked back at Rosy. "I don't think we have to go anywhere today," he said. "We can stay close to camp, and not leave tracks all over the mountain."

"That's fine," she answered. "I like it here."

Pete looked off in the direction of the Throne of Seven Cedars, as he thought he would call the spot. It wasn't visible from camp, but he could picture it well enough. He imagined it was pretty dry inside. It would be nice to go back there, but for right now it was better not to track up the snow.

They had a leisurely morning with breakfast and then coffee. After a silence of several minutes, Pete spoke up. "There was somethin' you said yesterday that's got me curious."

"And what is that?"

"Well, you said you wanted to wait until marriage."

"Of course. That's the way it's supposed to be."

"Well, yeah, I knew that. I guess the part I wanted to ask about was what your outlook was. I take it you expect to get married some day. Now that I think of it, I believe you even mentioned it before, when you talked about your dad." He looked at her.

She met him with her eyes. "Yes, I do. It's something we all look forward to. With my people, you know. It's our dream, to have our own house and family."

"What kind of a man do you think it'll be?" He pictured a light-featured man like himself and a dark-featured man, both in hats and boots and spurs.

"Oh," she said, pursing her lips and then relaxing them, "someone who understands me and treats me well. No one wants a man who drinks too much or hits her. And I wouldn't want someone who was always fighting with other men."

It wasn't the kind of answer he was fishing for, but it was good to find out about. "Let me put it another way." He was looking at the fire now. "Do you have it in your mind that this fellow'll be like you?" He looked back up at her.

She gave him a quizzical look. "How?"

"I mean, your own kind. Or would you ever look at someone like me?"

She laughed. "I should pinch you. Aren't you a person too?"

He looked at the fire again. "Yeah, but it scared the hell out of me to have to ask." He looked back at her. "I'm not askin' for any guarantees, but if we get out of this thing free, would you at least look at me in that way?"

Her eyes sparkled. "Do you think I would let you kiss me if I didn't?"

He could see a little of the coquette in her, and he laughed. "No, I bet you wouldn't." Then he leaned over and kissed her quick, right then.

"Be careful," she said, smiling.

"Oh, I will." He remembered the feeling he

had had the day before, with his back to the open world as he lost himself in her kiss. At her playful warning now to be careful, he remembered he really did have reasons to be on his guard. It would be a sad business if he lost himself in kissy-kiss and let the King come sneaking up behind him at the Throne of Seven Cedars. He gave a half shudder. Then he smiled at her and winked. "I'll be careful." He gave a look around. "In more ways than one."

The weather was clearing off, which meant that some of the snow might melt, and then with the clear skies of night it could freeze. That could make for a crust in the thick spots and ice in the exposed areas. A moonlit night, with a full snow on the ground, also had good visibility for traveling. They had surprised his camp at dawn once before, and even though this one should be harder to find, they could do it again—if they didn't do it before.

In the afternoon he built the fire again, and they cooked a meal. Cedar wood made good campfires, but sometimes it gave off black smoke as it did now. It seemed to Pete that smells carried better over snow, and he wondered from how far off the black smoke could be seen. Worry was setting in and he wasn't sure why, but he thought it would be best not to have a fire after dark.

The next morning broke cold and clear. When Pete went out to check the horses and move them, he noticed there had been some melt and freezing but not much. The snow had a very thin crust, and it still formed a solid blanket across the mountainside. He decided that after breakfast he would take Star for a ride, so as not to leave human footprints, and see what kind of movement there had been in the vicinity. It would be a short ride, and he could go bareback.

He brought the rifle out of the tent and kept it handy where he had the saddles stacked. If something down below didn't happen by today, he should be hearing from Pearl.

He built a little fire and used canteen water for coffee. He didn't feel like playing the game of gathering and melting snow. Time and again he scanned the country and looked down at the horses, but nothing seemed out of order.

Rosy pushed open the tent flap and stepped out into the cold morning. She gave a short, closed-mouth smile as she signaled with her thumb and forefinger that she would be back in a little bit.

Pete nodded and returned to kneel by the fire. It was going to be really tight. He would get back to Laramie barely in time to meet his party of dudes. The camp outfit was already lined up, but he would still have to buy grub and make up the packs. He hoped he had this other business cleared up by then. It wouldn't do to have to watch his back while he was minding a group of newcomers. Four of them—that would be a handful.

He picked up a cedar stick, held it with both hands, and put his knee against the midpoint. Then he decided not to make the noise; he could burn the stick in half. He was relaxing the tension when he heard Rosy scream.

Pete was on his feet with the rifle in his left hand, running towards the sound, before he even knew it. Then he cautioned himself. If there was more than one man out there, he could run right into a bullet. She had screamed, which meant they were doing something like before. Last time they had gone around him. This time they might be hoping to lure him. He stopped.

He knew there was a little clump of aspens she went to. That's where it would be easiest to nab her. The aspens would cut off some line of fire, but they would make a good spot for someone to be waiting for him.

He thought of a better way to go. It would take a couple of minutes longer, but he could come out of some trees on the other side of the spot where she had headed. He ran, bending low, hearing the soft crunch of his boots in the snow. He was in pines now, forty yards below camp. He ran softer, not wanting to get himself breathing too hard to make a steady shot. Then he came to a set of tracks—one man's tracks. That was good. He followed the tracks to the edge of the timber and looked out across the mountainside.

There was a dark form with part of it thrashing. It was the form of a man, tall in comparison with Rosy, holding her off the ground. It looked like Gregory, but Pete couldn't be sure. The man was wearing a dark wool military overcoat, and instead of a hat he wore a fur cap that looked like coyote. Turned partially away from Pete, he seemed to hold Rosy with his right arm, elevating her with his right hip. With his left hand he was shaking out a rope.

Pete stuffed his gloves in his coat pocket, found a steady rest against a pine tree, and settled his sights onto the man. It was about a hundred yards. *Aim for the middle*, he told himself. An overcoat like that would be like a coyote's fur in winter, making the target seem larger than it was. Aim for the center, and make one good shot when it was clear.

He eased off and took a deep breath. No good to hold steady for too long. The man wasn't getting very far, and now he was looking over his left shoulder towards camp. Still Rosy struggled, and it looked grotesque—as if two people were joined at the hip, and one of them wanted to get free while the other one tried to prevent it.

Then the man slammed her on the ground, put his foot on her, and straightened up to get both hands on the rope. Pete took dead center aim and fired.

The man lurched and ran straight away, then turned and veered downhill for several strides and finally plunged forward in the snow.

Pete levered in another shell. There was still a good shot if he needed it. The form didn't move. Pete waited a long moment, then stepped out of the timber, crouching and then running towards Rosy.

She was lying on the ground, snow in her hair and on her coat. Her upper body was heaving up and down in heavy breaths.

Pete came to a kneeling stop, looking at her but trying to keep an eye on the other form laid out in the snow. He put a hand on her shoulder. "Are you all right?"

She looked up, pain on her face as she trembled. "I think so."

"Is that him? The third man?"

"Yes," she said. "The one with the horses."

"I'll be back," he said. He patted her shoulder and raised into a crouch.

With his rifle in front of him he approached the form, circling up the hill to stay at its back. He imagined that if he went straight to it and rolled the body over, Gregory could surprise him at short range with a six-gun from underneath the coat. Pete shook his head.

As he walked forward he kept his eye out for a white mound that might be a loose rock. After kicking at a couple he rolled one loose, and carrying the rock in his left hand and the rifle in his right, he walked up to the foot of the body.

It was lying face down with the right arm out and the right knee drawn up. The coat was spread out on the right side, unbuttoned. The left hand could be holding a gun under that coat.

Pete dropped the rock on the man's knee. No movement. He stepped on the left calf, and again there was no reaction. Only then did he stand over the corpse and roll it back by the shoulder. The first thing that caught his eye was the wide red stain on the snow. He had made a good shot. Then he moved his gaze from the wet shirt to the face, and he knew for sure. It was Logan Gregory. The gatekeeper was on ice.

Chapter Sixteen

After Pete had gotten Rosy back to camp, he dragged the body down into the timber. As he pulled on the rope he recalled the times he had been in Gregory's presence, when the other man had reason to kill him but didn't. Pete wondered why. That day on the ledge overlooking the holding pen, Gregory was obviously working for the Mrs. He had been so sure of himself, he must have imagined he could take Pete whenever he wanted in his own good time, in a way that would please the boss but not come to the attention of the Mrs. Or maybe he just wanted to get his hands on Rosy and leave Pete for the King. That was possible, too. Either way, Gregory had been too sure. Like Chicago Thorne, maybe he had been smarter than Pete, but in the long run he was too smart for his own good. His overconfidence was his own undoing—that was how it looked now.

Pete wondered how smart the man was about himself. He thought he was his own master, but he clearly wasn't. If he hadn't been working for the King, he wouldn't have had to worry about a servant girl who could put a finger on him. He had probably been content to hold the horses that day in the thicket because he knew he had his own kootchie-koo waiting for him back at the castle, but if he hadn't been working for the Mrs., he could have taken care of Pete Garnett long ago.

The wool coat slid well on the snow. Pete laid the body out on its back and straightened the coat over the chest and bloody shirt. At that moment he thought to look at the neck. Gregory was wearing a red neckerchief, which Pete lifted. There was the leather thong. Pete wondered if Gregory had dressed that carefully to make it more difficult for Pete and Rosy to compare details. As for the key, whatever closet or strongbox it might have controlled would now have to be opened by other hands. Pete dropped the knotted neckerchief, stood up, and turned away.

He decided to leave the rope where it lay sunken out of sight in the snow. Somewhere back in the timber there was probably a horse tied up, but Pete preferred not to worry about that detail until he had an idea of where the

King was. The King could be out of the way already, he could be in the hoosegow, or he could be somewhere else on the mountain, wondering about the lone shot he heard after he split up from Gregory. The strength of the last possibility quickened Pete's steps back to camp.

Rosy was sitting huddled by the fire, but she wasn't shivering like she had been. She gave Pete a questioning look as he sat down next to her.

"You don't have to worry about that one any more," he said, patting her hand.

"He was so strong," she said. "It was like iron. He told me if I screamed again he would break my neck."

"Well, he's gone for good. The only one left to worry about is the kingpin, but that's a big worry." He saw that she had coffee, so he poured some for himself. The top of the pyramid—that's what the King was. The lower levels were laid out like blocks of stone, and here they were, he and Rosy, waiting at the top to do or die. "I don't like just sitting here," he said, "but if we move camp we'll be just as easy to find. This snow would make us as plain as Hansel and Gretel with a pocketful of rocks." He looked at her. "Do you know that story?"

She shook her head.

"I'll tell it to you sometime." He took out his tobacco, and as he rolled the cigarette he saw that his hands were trembling. He looked at Rosy and saw that she was watching. "I think we'd just as well stay put. But when I finish this cigarette, I think I'll bring the horses in closer. You can come with me."

She nodded. This last encounter with Gregory had clearly scared her more than the previous two.

"Don't worry, Rosy. We'll get out of this all right." Even as he said it he knew he was whistling in the dark. The King could be anywhere.

"I know," she said, and her voice sounded more convincing to him than his own did.

He smoked his cigarette down to a snipe and tossed it in the fire. She had finished her coffee, so he tossed down the rest of his and stood up. He looked at the rifle leaning against the saddles and decided it would be too clumsy if he was going to lead the three horses. Rosy could carry it back, but he didn't want to put that burden on her right now. He touched his pistol with his right hand and held out his left to help her to her feet. She kept his hand as they sauntered out of camp.

They hadn't gone fifteen paces when Pete heard a voice at his back. It merely said, "Stop."

Stop they did.

"Now turn around. Slow."

Pete knew the voice, knew there could be only one person after them at this point. Now that person had the drop on them. Pete thought of trying something, but he knew it would be bad judgment with Rosy so close. Pete let go of her hand and turned around slowly to face the

King. Rosy turned at the same time and stood at Pete's right.

The King stood uphill from them, and he towered over them in a fur overcoat and black hat. Beneath the overcoat was his customary black outfit, with the watch chain shining in the sun. He held a rifle pointed at the young couple. "I've been waiting quite a while for this rendezvous with you, you little dunce."

Pete felt like saying, "I know. Your wife told me." But he said nothing. He knew the man could fly into a rage, and this was no time for the door to open.

The King shifted his gaze toward Rosy. "And you, my little pearblossom. We meet for the first time." His eyes went hard. "Now you lift that sidegun out of his holster, and you throw it over here in the snow."

Pete felt his holster pull upward against his hip, and then he saw his revolver disappear into the snow in front of him.

"Now," said the King, "we've got all day. No need to hurry the pleasure. I'm sorry Logan can't join us." The slate-grey eyes turned upon Pete. "You did me a favor, boy. I thought I was going to have to put him away when the party was over, but it looks like you did."

"I had to."

"I can't say that I think he didn't deserve it. You know, I have a wife, and I think my man was"—the grey eyes flickered toward Rosy and back—"long-arming me. Isn't that a disgrace?"

247

"If you say so."

"I do. So I thank you for the favor." The King smiled. "But I'm going to kill you anyway." The smile faded. "You know I have reasons."

"If you say so."

"Don't mock me, or you'll make me hurry my pleasure. I want to tell you something."

"I'm listening."

"I thought so. First, I want to tell you that the man you killed at the Edwards Hotel was a dear friend of mine. He was like a brother and father both."

Pete nodded. He felt a chill run through him.

"Second, I want to tell you that I've had you in my rifle sights two other times before today."

Pete shivered, as if his blood had run to ice water.

"And you know why I didn't squeeze the trigger?"

"No."

"Because I'm too much of a gentleman to shoot even a scrub like you in the back." The King snickered. "Not when I can laugh in your face and prolong the pleasure."

Pete felt Rosy's hand in his. He squeezed it.

"Let go of her," said the King. "I have some use for her—yes, you—as soon as I'm done with you, Garnett. But I wanted you to know that, too, before you go. And don't worry about her. When I'm done with her, I'll put her in a place where little girls can't talk."

Pete heard the click of a rifle followed by another voice. "I don't think so."

Pete looked back to his left, and there was Pearl in a sheepskin coat, stepping out of the campsite. He must have followed Gregory and the King up the mountain. His voice was curt. "Drop the rifle, Flagg."

The King raised his eyebrows and lifted his head. "I wouldn't want to—" And then with lightning swiftness he rotated the rifle at his hips and sent a shot at Pearl.

The old horse trader jerked backwards and flung his rifle forward into the snow. In that moment, Pete turned and ran for the timber.

Rosy ran with him, and he told her, "Run that way!" as he pointed to his left and went on to his right, crouching and zigzagging. Pete knew the King would shoot at him, so her getaway was assured for the moment.

Two shots whined past him, with the rifle booming in the background. Pete reached the edge of the dark timber, jumped over a deadfall, and dove into cover. He looked to his left and saw movement. Rosy had made it to the timber, also. Pete turned around on his hands and knees. He could hear Rosy run deeper into the trees, and he could see the King standing where he had been, looking down their way and thumbling new cartridges into the rifle.

Pete looked to the left and could see Pearl's coat in the snow. "I'm sorry, Pearl," he whispered. Now he forgave his old friend for being so quick to shoot Thorne. If he had done it again, this nightmare would be over, but he must have had second thoughts about Thorne after all. As it was, there were only two ways out. Pete bit his lip. The King could find him, or Pete could get to his rifle first.

Pete looked back at the King. He seemed to have caught sight of the horses and was taking slow steps to get a vantage point on them. It looked as if the King intended to cut off any getaway.

Pete began moving to his left. If he could move around the contour of the hill, he might be able to get to camp without being seen. If he could get to his rifle, he would have a chance. But if the King got to the camp first, he could freeze them out.

The King turned and walked back towards the camp and took up a position midway between it and the horses. That was going to make it harder.

Then Pete remembered a detail he had set aside earlier. Gregory's horse would be out here somewhere, and it was bound to have a saddle gun strapped onto it. All Pete had to do was backtrail where Gregory came in. He could do that from deeper in the timber.

He moved quickly, and a shot came crashing through the trees. His heart jumped, and he ducked and dodged and kept running. Then he thought, it was next to impossible for anyone to make that kind of shot downhill through timber. The King just wanted to pin him down.

He kept going, farther than he expected, until he found the trail. He had gotten turned partway in the woods and had been running almost parallel to the trail. Now he followed it on out, covering three of the dead man's steps with every two of his own strides. In less than half a mile he came to it, the sorrel horse he had seen Gregory ride, and there in the boot was what he was looking for.

Might as well use the horse, too, he thought. He untied it and swung aboard. The horse was well rested, and in a short time it could bring him up and around in back of the King.

Pete was still shaking when he slid out of the saddle and tied the sorrel horse to a pine branch. Now it was really do or die. He needed to find out where his man was, and he needed to make one good shot.

He sidehilled to the crest of the mountain. Camp and the horses would be down to the left. The sun was in his eyes so he pulled down his hat brim. Then, cradling the rifle, he duckwalked to a rock and looked over. He could see the horses and he could see the tent through the trees it sat up against, but he could not see the man he was looking for.

Then he saw smoke rising from the campsite. It looked like smoke from a fire being built up, not the wisp of a fire burning down. The King must be helping himself to a cup of coffee and congratulating himself for having found Pete's rifle.

Now he needed a decoy to bring the King out into the open. He thought of the sorrel horse. He could bring it to the top and turn it loose, and it would probably go down to the other horses. The King would recognize it and take interest. It was likely his horse that Gregory had been riding. It was worth a try.

He made it back to the horse in a short while and rode it to the top as planned. Dismounting, he took off his belt and whipped the horse on the rump to send it downhill. It worked. The sorrel horse headed towards the other horses. Then it turned, trotted back to the top, and crossed the ridge behind the camp.

Well enough. Here came the King, his rifle cradled in his arm, coming up the hill and turning to his left to follow the horse's tracks. Pete was crouched again behind a rock with the rifle ready, but there was too much snow on the rock to lay the gun on it. He would have to rise and fire.

Up the hill he came now, a bearded man in a fur coat, step by step. It would be a sideways shot unless Pete could get him to turn. Now.

"Rex!" he called out.

The King straightened up and turned, like a buck deer with a crown of antlers, as Pete stood up with the rifle aimed and pulled the trigger. Gregory's rifle shattered the mountain air, and the King fell backwards, clutching his rifle, as the echoes cascaded through the timber and canyons below.

Careful, Pete thought. *Make sure.* He ducked below the ridge, ran fifty yards to the north, and looked up over again.

There was the King, laid out with his head downhill and his hat in the snow behind him. The fur coat lay open, and the watch chain glinted in the sun.

Pete kept his man covered nevertheless until he came close enough to look down and be sure. The King was dead.

Pete walked around him and headed towards camp. As he sidestepped down through the snow, he thought of Lenore, the Mrs. She would be free now. True, she would be missing her helper, but if she had enlisted him mainly for his help in escaping, which seemed to be the case, she would be able to get by. Pete saw her as an attractive, intelligent woman who would probably not waste away. She might have her faults but she deserved another chance. She had come out of it better than Pearl had.

Pete needed to find Rosy, but first he felt he should pay his respects to Pearl. He walked over to the spot where the grey-bearded man lay face down with his hat cock-eyed over his face. It was too bad. He remembered how Pearl had wanted to have a kid some day, and now he wouldn't because he had stepped in to save Pete and Rosy.

"I'm sorry, Pearl," he said.

The grey beard moved as the muffled words came out. "Don't stand there being sorry. Help me get this hole plugged up."

Pete knelt immediately. "Pearl! I thought you were a goner!" He set the hat aside and looked into the blue eyes.

There was pain on the older man's face. "So did I," he said, "but I just laid here so he wouldn't shoot me again. I'd rather bleed to death."

"He must have walked right past you."

"I heard footsteps in the snow. Then I heard 'em goin' back, and I heard a shot. Then I heard these steps right now. Yours. Did you kill the sonofabitch?"

"Yes, I did."

"Good. I didn't think I could get up and do it." Pearl breathed through his open mouth. "I should have plugged him right there." He breathed again, with his tongue at his lower lip. "I hope he didn't kill me. I've been layin' here for an hour and I ain't dead yet, but I sure don't feel good."

"Don't worry, Pearl. I'll take care of you."

By noontime, Pete had him wrapped up and propped against a saddle. The bullet had torn up two ribs on the left side, but it had taken more meat than blood. When Pete had him stable, he said he was going to look for Rosy.

He met her at the edge of the timber, where he took her in his arms and she clung to him just as tight.

"It's over," he said. "We're free."

He took her hand, and together they walked up the mountain. *Free*, he thought. Free to live. Free to join his life with hers and to return some day to the Throne of Seven Cedars.